THE ROGUE
ELEMENT

THE ROGUE
ELEMENT

A SCOTT PRIEST MYSTERY

JOHN HARDY BELL

SECOND
SIGHT
PUBLISHING

This is a work of fiction. All of the organizations, characters, and events portrayed in this novel are either products of the author's imagination or are used fictitiously.

For more, visit www.johnhardybell.com

For THE PUSHER

THE ROGUE
ELEMENT

The law does not pretend to punish everything that is dishonest. That would seriously interfere with business.

~ *Charles Darrow*

CHAPTER 1

The presidential suite where Marisol Alvarez spent her last moments of life was the most elaborate residence that the Four Seasons Hotel had to offer. Measuring in at over 2,200 square feet, it was nearly triple the size of my apartment, with more amenities in the kitchen alone than in all the DPD district stations combined. It's rare to get a first-hand view of vacation accommodations that are reserved strictly for the one-percent (unless you're in the one-percent of course) and I had to catch my breath more than once as I walked through the door. The warm fuzzies lasted until I caught sight of the dense blood spatter covering most of the living room floor and furniture. After that, the place wasn't nearly as appealing.

The call came in a little after five this morning, just as I was mentally preparing to make a pre-work trip that I wasn't looking forward to. I'd secretly hoped that something would come up before I could make it to the assisted living facility where my once indestructible father fought to maintain what was left of the man he used to be. But this wasn't the diversion I had in mind.

Marisol had been stabbed seventeen times in all. The

medical examiner estimated that at least seven of those wounds were inflicted postmortem. Typical in a crime of passion scenario. Defensive cuts on her arms, palms, and thighs pointed to a struggle, which meant that she probably saw her attacker coming and had time to react. Unfortunately, her reaction wasn't enough to prevent the severing of her carotid artery, the wound that most likely killed her.

Despite the blind rage that fueled Marisol's assailant, they were clear-minded enough to keep traces of themselves to a minimum. Aside from a bloody partial shoeprint on the marble floor of the bathroom where a fellow attendant found her half-naked body, there was nothing left behind to tie anyone else to the scene: no fingerprints, no visible DNA, and no murder weapon.

The lack of physical evidence was just one of the early obstacles my partner Nathan Kimball and I were facing. The lack of a motive was another. Marisol had worked in the hotel for only eight days, barely enough time to learn the layout of the rooms she was responsible for cleaning. If she'd made enemies during her time here, she did so quickly and without any fanfare. None of the staff interviewed so far claimed to know her before she was hired. Most hadn't spoken two words to her since. From what we could gather, there was nothing at all remarkable about the thirty-seven-year-old Denver native, other than the fact that someone wanted her dead in the most brutal way imaginable.

"I'd certainly label this as excessive," Kimball said as he bent down to inspect the six puncture wounds on her back. "You don't go through this kind of effort unless you really want to punish someone."

"The fact that he dragged her body through the suite and dumped her face down into the bathtub also meant that he wanted to humiliate her," I added. "This was obviously someone she knew."

Kimball nodded as he stood up. "Looks like the relationship took a sour turn." His sharp brown face suddenly contorted with distress. "You mind if we step out for a bit? I'm starting to get that stomach thing again."

Like most detectives I knew, myself included, Kimball couldn't stand the sight of blood for very long. The human in you never gets used to a crime scene, no matter how often you step inside one. The jaded cop in you claims that it merely comes with the territory. Thankfully, we were both more human than jaded cop.

After each taking a drink from the water bottles we'd brought in, Kimball and I reconvened in the kitchen, the only space in the suite not currently occupied by CSIs and crime-scene photographers.

"How many rooms does the hotel have?" I asked.

"Two-hundred and fifty."

"That's a lot of doors to knock on."

"We've got some uniforms on standby in the lobby. They can start on the first floor and work their way up."

I shook my head at the mere thought of the logistical nightmare ahead of us. "How long before all that knocking starts panicking the guests?"

"There could still be a killer somewhere in the building. They should be panicked."

"Let's minimize that if we can. Without knowing what we're dealing with, we have to make sure the canvassers keep their questions basic."

Kimball nodded his agreement. "I'll radio them to come up for a briefing."

I knew the chance of a hotel guest providing anything useful was slim at best, but we had to try. We'd already questioned most of the overnight staff, and none of them could place Marisol anywhere in the hotel, even though she was scheduled to report at four A.M today. Her shirt was similar to the uniforms worn by other staff, so we were confident she was here for work. But according to the cleaning schedule, she wasn't assigned to the presidential suite. That assignment went to another attendant, the one who had the misfortune of finding her. So, what was Marisol doing in here?

Before I could attempt to formulate an answer, we were joined by a CSI named Robert Franklin, a six-foot-six-inch mountain of a human being who also happened to play offensive guard for the same Colorado State Rams football team as my esteemed partner. If I was Kimball's best friend in the department, Franklin was running a very close second. "Morning, gentlemen. Helluva wake-up call, huh?"

"The worst," Kimball said. "But you can make it all better by telling us you have the perp downstairs in handcuffs."

Franklin's bearded face curled up in a half-smile. "No such luck, Kimmy. Looks like you're stuck doing your job for a while longer."

Kimball turned to me. "Does this guy ever deliver good news?"

"Sorry to break it to you, but bad news is our specialty."

"As usual, Scott is the only one between you two who actually gets it," Franklin said with a light laugh. "I hope you realize how lucky you are to have him."

"I thank my lucky stars every day," Kimball responded with a hint of sarcasm. "Now get to the bad news."

"We just heard from the hotel general manager Natalie Glassman. She's insisting that we hold off on questioning any of the guests until she gets here."

"That's fine," I said. "How long until she arrives?"

"She's been in Los Angeles for a conference and was en route to LAX to jump an emergency flight when we spoke. It could be a while."

"Isn't that just perfect," Kimball muttered through clenched teeth. "Anything else?"

"Apparently, the cameras on this floor and the three floors below malfunctioned last night, so the hotel security guys can't pull up any footage. They've called in a tech to try and diagnose the problem, but it's going to set us back a couple more hours."

Overcome with frustration, Kimball could only shake his head. "I love you Rob, but you're really bad for morale."

"Where are we at with forensics?" I followed up.

"We've got teams scattered throughout the hotel looking inside every trash bin and dumpster. If the perp left behind any evidence outside of the suite, we'll find it. But so far, goose-eggs."

I gave Franklin a pat on his broad shoulder. "We appreciate the work. And don't listen to our friend here. You're great for morale."

"Ah, the joy of being appreciated," Franklin quipped with a loud sigh. "Take notes, Detective Kimball."

Kimball rolled his eyes, feigning annoyance as best he could. "Whatever. Just make sure you find my murder weapon."

Franklin bowed in mock deference. "I'm all over it, boss." With that, he walked away to rejoin the other CSIs in the bathroom.

"Looks like we're officially in limbo," Kimball said. "I guess we can go dumpster-diving with forensics if we really want to pass some time."

My thoughts abruptly landed on my father. "Do you think you can handle that on your own?"

Kimball's brow furrowed. "You got something better to do?"

"I promised my mom that I'd go visit dad this morning. Apparently, he's really looking forward to seeing me. I find that hard to believe, but she insists it's true. I'd try and reschedule, but the doctors say the best way to keep him engaged is to maintain a regular schedule of events around his day, and I'm next up on the schedule. I didn't think I'd make it there, but now that we have this lull..."

Kimball's firm expression immediately softened. "Say no more. You go see your old man. Rob's crew can hold it down until the hotel manager makes it in."

"I'll be back as soon as I can," I said, thankful for Kimball's understanding.

"Take your time, Scott. Family comes first. You just make sure to tell your mom that I'm gonna need another one of her famous pumpkin pies ASAP."

She enjoyed making those pies for Nate just as much as he enjoyed eating them. It didn't hurt that he was the only one ever to make the request. "I'll be sure to pass along the message."

"After I get the canvassers up to speed, I'll head back to HQ to start the paperwork, so let's meet up there when you're finished. Krieger and Parsons are assisting, so if anything breaks while you're gone, they can manage it until we come back."

"Will do. And thanks again."

"Not a problem." Kimball's eyes grew heavy. "Good luck."

If the first few visits were any indication of what was to come, I'd need all the luck I could get. "Thank you."

I took in a deep breath when I stepped out of the suite. The smell of heavy copper had taken up residence in my nose, and it felt good to cleanse it with fresh air.

I passed a convoy of uniformed officers on my way to the elevator and instantly felt guilty that I wasn't with Kimball. But I had another job to attend to – the job of being Carl Priest's son. It was a thankless position with lousy hours, few benefits, and a whole lot of expectations that I couldn't possibly fulfill. But given the current dynamics of my family, being dutiful was much more important than being happy. I never knew how he would react to seeing me, but that still didn't change the fact that he needed me. And as challenging as the job of being my father's only surviving son was, I needed him too.

CHAPTER 2

Carl Priest was a senior detective with the DPD narcotics unit for over nineteen years. He spent six years as a patrol officer before that, and another eight in Major Crimes. His record for arrests leading to a successful conviction was second to none. He was also a larger than life character whose formidable physical presence was matched only by his razor-sharp skill as an investigator. His hard-nosed, no-nonsense approach continues to be the gold standard for a narcotics unit in which he is practically deified, and I'm confident that it's only a matter of time before they lobby for some sort of statue in his honor.

The man sitting before me in his plain-white Oxford shirt, pleated khakis, and green cardigan sweater looked nothing like a god. He looked more like someone who should be reading nursery rhymes to a roomful of squirmy five-year-old's. The thick bifocals that continually slid off the bridge of his narrow nose certainly would've made the task easier.

"Why would you swing that hard with a goddamned nine-iron?" he asked the overweight man on the plasma television who was giving golf tips that my father would never get the chance to use. "You're not driving it off the tee for god's sake."

He was so absorbed in the program, I wasn't sure that he even noticed when I walked in. If he did notice, he wasn't moved enough by my presence to acknowledge it. Rather than scurry for his attention, I took the opportunity to catch up with my mother.

Ellen Priest may have been the only one of us who actually lived up to the surname. She's a saint if I've ever known one. Being a cop's wife forces you to be stronger than most. Being the mother of two more cops makes you superhuman in your capacity to deal with the curveballs that life can throw at you. She dealt with more than her share of curveballs, including the nightmare of losing her eldest son, my big brother, in the line of duty. But she handled it all with more grace and courage than a human being should ever be allowed to possess. She held our little family together through the most devastating of storms, even if it was often by the thinnest of threads, yet she rarely asked for, or received the acknowledgment that she deserved. And now she was losing her husband of forty-two years; not to an enemy that he encountered on the street, but to an enemy that he encountered in the very core of his being. And there was nothing anyone could do to stop it. These visits were as much about supporting her as they were about my father. I'm certain she still doesn't hear 'thank you' nearly as much as she should, so I take every opportunity I can to say it.

"Do you need me to come by the house and do anything?" I asked her as we huddled near the front door. "The weather is starting to warm up, and I know the yard can get unruly. It's been a while, but I think I still know my way around a lawnmower."

"Not necessary," my mom answered with the gentle smile that had probably been her trademark since birth. "I hired a guy to take care of it."

"That's good. But if you need anything else done around there, I'm only a phone call away. I know I can work crazy hours, but I'm off a lot during the day. It wouldn't be a problem at all." I was trying too hard, and I knew she could sense it. A reassuring pat on the chest was enough to tell me it would be okay.

"From what they're saying on TV, you've got your hands full as it is. The entire department does."

"You can't believe everything you hear on TV, mom."

"In this case, I hope that's true."

Eager to change the subject, I turned an eye to my father. He was still captivated by the big guy and his terrible golf swing. "How's dad?"

She took a shallow breath and held it in. "You know, good days and bad days."

"Are there more of one than the other?"

"Sixty-forty bad."

A wave of guilt washed over me. I'd always feared that I hadn't come around nearly enough. Now I knew it for sure. "You have to tell me if it gets to be too much. I'll drop everything to be there for you."

"It's fine, Scotty. Hell, sometimes it's worse on the good days." The quiet laugh we shared immediately broke the tension. "Will you go talk to him now? I don't know how much more of this stupid golf show I can stomach listening to."

I nodded, knowing my stall tactic had officially run its course. "Dad's watched that same guy for years. Apparently, some things will never change, no matter what. That's a good thing, right?"

Her brown eyes briefly lost focus, as if a heavy thought had taken her someplace far away. When she came back, she looked sad. "I've convinced myself of that too, sweetheart."

Dad's gaze didn't move away from the TV as I pulled up a chair next to his recliner and sat, though the tense shift in his body language told me that he'd been somewhat annoyed at the intrusion. After a few seconds of uncomfortable silence, he finally said, "Does this mean I have to turn off the TV now?"

"That's exactly what it means, Carl," my mom said from across the room. "The damn thing's been on all morning. Your son is very busy, and he took time out of his day to come and see you. Turning off that idiot box is the least you can do."

She was the only person in the history of the world who was able to consistently put Carl Priest in his place without an ounce of pushback, as evidenced by his quick work with the remote.

"I know he's busy," he countered, the suddenly quiet space absorbing the full weight of his strong tone. "He's a dedicated cop. Dedicated cops stay busy." He finally turned to me. "Isn't that right, Scotty?"

Intimidated by him as I always was, I couldn't hold his stare for long. "The work never lets up."

The good news was that he seemed to be fully present today. Depending on his mood, that could've also been the bad news.

"Working anything interesting?"

I nodded. "A hotel room attendant. She was–"

"Do I want to hear about this?" my mom quickly interrupted. The answer was always the same anytime I brought up work.

"Definitely not."

"In that case, I'll exit stage left so you two can talk shop," she said as she promptly picked up her purse and car keys.

"Where are you going?" my dad asked, his eyes glazing over with a fear that troubled me.

"Don't worry, I'll be back. I'm just going to the store to pick up a few things."

His eyes quickly returned to normal. "Oh, well then, could you pick up some of those cashews that I like? And a six-pack of Coors?"

"The cashews are already on my list. Nice try with the beer, pal."

A trace of a smile crossed my father's lips, an anomaly that I wouldn't witness again for the rest of the visit.

"I'll be back soon," my mother reported. "Love you, Scotty."

"Love you too, mom."

Dad stared at the door for a long time after she left.

After a bout of silence, I finally asked: "Pretty nice place you've set up here. How are you adjusting to it?"

"I miss being home," he answered, still staring at the door.

His sudden vulnerability threw me, and I was stuck for a response. "You never know, things could get better, and you could go back." I regretted saying that the moment it came out of my mouth.

His narrow eyes burrowed into me. "Things aren't going to get better, Scott."

Even though I knew that was true, hearing it from him made the reality even more painful. "How about we just take it day by day."

His eyes landed on the door again. "That's all I can do." After another silence, he turned back to me. "So, about that case."

The buzz of my cell phone interrupted me before I could answer. I picked it up and was surprised to see Lieutenant Owen Hitchcock's office number. I assumed he was calling about Marisol Alvarez and decided I could fill him in later. I stuffed the phone back into my pocket without giving it a second thought.

"Who was that?" dad asked.

"Work. Nothing that can't wait."

He nodded. "So, was she killed in the hotel?"

"The room attendant? Yes. Inside the Four Seasons Presidential Suite."

"Talk about going out in style. You have any suspects?"

"Not yet. We've interviewed most of the staff and we're getting to the guests soon. No one even saw her come into the hotel, so for now, we're still at square one."

"It was probably one of the staff."

"That's what we're thinking."

"How was she killed?"

"She was–" My cell phone rang again. Hitchcock.

When dad asked who it was, I told him. His expression hardened. "I can't believe that jerk-off is still in charge of homicide with everything happening there."

Eager to shift the focus, I answered his question about Marisol. "She was stabbed multiple times."

Dad paused to gather himself for the change in topic. "Stabbed, huh? The killer must've been someone she knew intimately. Probably a lover."

"We're assuming that too."

"That's nice. But assumptions don't solve cases. Tell me what you know."

I was pondering an answer when my phone vibrated. Hitchcock was now sending a text message. "For Christ's sake, what do you want?"

His message was short and sweet: *I need to see you in my office, ASAP.*

When I asked him if it was concerning the Alvarez case, he replied: *No.*

When I asked him if Kimball would be joining us, he replied: *No. Only you.*

My heart danced a little in my chest. Nothing like being called into the principal's office before the school day even starts.

"Hitchcock again?" my dad asked, appropriately irritated.

"Yes."

"What the hell is so urgent?"

I shrugged. "He wants to see me in his office ASAP."

"Does he want to talk to you and Nate about your case?"

"I don't know. But he only wants to see me."

Dad hissed.

"What?" I asked.

"You need to watch that guy."

"Lieutenant Hitchcock?"

"Yeah. I hope you're not putting too much trust in him."

"He's never given me a reason not to."

"He's a snake, Scotty. And I'm telling you for your own good not to trust him."

"Why you think he's a snake?"

He sat back in his chair and looked at the blank television. "I'd rather not get into it right now. Your mom will be back any minute. Just take my word for it."

I had no idea where this was coming from or how to respond, so I didn't say anything.

After yet another extended silence, he asked, "How's Nate?"

"Waiting impatiently for the day he gets to run the place. Same as always."

"Nate should be running things there." He turned back to me. "You've got a good friend in him. Make sure you focus on looking out for him and the other men in that unit."

"There are women in the unit too, dad."

"Save the PC crap. You know what I mean. Always make sure it's his back you're watching and not the weasels at the top. They only care about themselves, and when the shit hits the fan, which it always does, they'll throw you under the bus without a moment's hesitation."

Quite the pleasant visit this was turning out to be. "I always watch Nate's back."

Almost on cue, another text from Hitchcock came in. *Are you coming?*

This conversation had me on edge and the last thing I wanted was a meeting with Hitchcock, but I told him that I'd be there in twenty.

"Is he still hounding you?"

I nodded. "Looks like I have to go."

"I figured. Just remember what I said. It doesn't sit right that he only wants to have a meeting with you."

"Are you assuming he wants to meet with me about Nate?"

"I'm not assuming anything, just offering some general information based on experience."

"I'll take it under advisement," I said as I stood up.

"You do that. And about your case. Make sure you don't leave any stone unturned when it comes to the staff. I can almost guarantee that it's a guy who works there, which means catching him should be easy."

"I appreciate the vote of confidence."

"I didn't say you would catch him, I said it should be easy." One last dig for good measure.

I went in for a hug despite not wanting to. It was as awkward as I imagined it would be. "Will you be okay here until mom gets back?"

"Of course," he said proudly. When he turned on the TV, the big guy was still dishing out golf advice, only now he'd traded in his tight khakis for shorts and knee-high socks.

"Okay. You hang in there, dad. I'll be back to see you soon."

"Make sure you do. I'll be curious to hear about this meeting of yours, and the hotel maid, of course."

I was tempted to remind him that they weren't called maids anymore but saw no point. "You got it."

I'd just opened the door to walk out when he said something that stopped me dead in my tracks. "I used to be upset that you weren't more like your brother. But I see now that's a good thing. Matty took too many chances, just like I did. And it cost him everything. I know that won't happen to you."

I felt a jagged lump form in my throat that I struggled to swallow. "It won't."

"Good. Just be smart Scotty. And stay out of the tall weeds. Believe me, you won't like what's in there."

CHAPTER 3

I stood outside of Lieutenant Owen Hitchcock's office fighting like hell to keep down the bagel and cream cheese breakfast I'd grabbed on my way to HQ. My nerves were totally shot, and I wasn't sure why. I could only guess it was because I'd never been summoned for an early morning impromptu meeting with the lieutenant that didn't involve some impossible case I was slogging through. The conversation with my father didn't help.

Still worried that the contents of my stomach would have a hard time staying where they were supposed to, I knocked on the door; two quick raps to not draw too much attention. Why I cared that anyone saw me standing outside the lieutenant's office was a question I couldn't answer. I only knew that I cared.

I took in a hard breath. Before I could exhale, I heard Hitchcock's muffled voice.

"Come in."

I walked into the cramped office and quickly shut the door behind me. A man who was not Owen Hitchcock sat behind the lieutenant's desk. He wore a plain white shirt with a plain black tie. No suit jacket. His short-cropped brown hair was cut with military precision. A bureaucrat if I'd ever seen one. And he definitely wasn't from around here. His eager eyes burrowed into me as if he'd been anticipating this moment for a long time. Otherwise, he was expressionless.

Lieutenant Hitchcock stood to my right near the door, his wiry six-foot-three frame taking up nearly half the office space. He smiled; something he didn't do on his best day. And suddenly the gymnastics in my stomach started up again.

"Thanks for coming," was how he began the conversation.

The bureaucrat's eyes were still eager.

"It sounded urgent."

"It is."

Hitchcock pointed to the chair opposite his desk, and I promptly sat, avoiding further eye contact with the stranger sitting across from me.

The lieutenant continued. "I know it's a busy time, so I promise to make this as brief as possible."

"Brief is always good," I said before I could stop myself.

The lieutenant and his guest exchanged a glance. Hitchcock smiled again.

"Detective Scott Priest, this is Robert Fitzgerald. He's visiting us from the State Attorney General's office."

Attorney General's office. At least I was right about him being a bureaucrat. "Pleasure to meet you, Mr. Fitzgerald." My smile was more rigid than usual.

"Likewise, Detective Priest. I've heard a lot about you."

"Good things I hope."

"Nothing but." His lifeless tone said otherwise.

Determined to put an end to the forced pleasantries before they got out of hand, I turned to Hitchcock with my best *why in the hell am I here* look. Thankfully, he picked up on the cue.

"Don't let Mr. Fitzgerald's presence here alarm you, Scott."

"I'm not alarmed," which was a lie of course.

"Good, because there's no reason to be. When he said he'd heard nothing but positive things about you, that wasn't an exaggeration."

"I appreciate the vote of confidence, but that can't be why I'm here."

"Actually, it is."

"So, the AG is handing out commendations now?"

"No commendations. Not yet anyway."

The strained levity on my face morphed into frustration, and I sighed as I shifted in my chair. "With all due respect sir, I have a dead woman in a hotel suite and a lot of people I need to talk to about it. If this is something concerning a previous case or an administrative matter, maybe Detectives Krieger or Parsons would be better suited to—"

"We need your help, Scott, and it's got nothing to do with a case."

Even though I already knew as much, I had a difficult time masking my concern. "What does it have to do with?"

Hitchcock and Fitzgerald exchanged another glance as if they were both expecting the other to answer the question. When Fitzgerald crossed his arms and sank back in his chair, the lieutenant knew the task was his.

"I don't have to tell you how crazy it's been around here the past couple of months. It seems like every time I pull into the parking lot, the pool of reporters circling the building gets larger. They're looking to take giant chunks out of everyone's ass around here, and so far, they're succeeding. This business with the mayor's husband doesn't just have people upset. They want badges. Thirty years in the department and I can't remember a worse time to be here."

I shifted in my chair again, bracing for the uncomfortable territory I was about to find myself in.

The situation with Mayor Sonya Richmond and her husband Elliott made everyone around here uncomfortable. If we weren't hearing their names every night on the news, we were hearing it from nearly every private citizen we encountered on the street. And their opinions were rarely complimentary. These days, if someone spoke of the Denver Police Department, words like *murder, corrupt*, and *cover-up* were never far behind. The media hounds had already come to the collective conclusion that the allegations were true, without an ounce of credible evidence to back up their assertions. And once the media decided it was true, so did the public. Hitchcock was right; it wasn't a good time to be here.

He continued. "Latest word is that Elliott Richmond may be indicted on federal racketeering charges. As far as the other accusations that are being thrown out there, no one knows where that's headed yet."

"Not even the AG's office?" I asked the man occupying my boss's chair.

"All I can tell you is that we're working on it. But we're still a long way from where we want to be."

"Which is where you come in," Hitchcock said.

My chest felt heavy. "I'm not following."

Fitzgerald spoke. "Despite the situation with her husband, the mayor has been pushing for a thorough investigation into the rumors of rogue recruitment within the department. The top brass is saying all the right things, but there's reason to suspect at least some level of complicity from within those ranks."

"Explain what you mean by complicity."

"That's not relevant to this conversation," the bureaucrat insisted.

"I disagree, Mr. Fitzgerald. I'm not exactly sure what information you're sitting on, but the people in that unit, myself included, don't have the first clue about what's happening around here. We do know that some hired gun pretending to be a fellow officer shot two detectives we were all close to, but nobody seems to be in a hurry to tell us why they were shot or who this so-called officer actually was. If we want any kind of update, we have to watch the news, and they're basically making stuff up anyway. So when you tell me that complicity in the top brass is irrelevant to this conversation, you're saying that it's acceptable for us to keep taking the heat for them. And if that's the case, then the rest of this meeting is going to be an enormous waste of everyone's time."

"That's the furthest thing from the truth," Hitchcock declared.

"Maybe from your standpoint, lieutenant. But I don't think the Attorney General here gives a damn about how bad it is for the average beat-walker right now."

"That's a rather pointed accusation, detective," Fitzgerald barked. "And an insulting one."

I'd just opened my mouth to respond in an inappropriate way when Hitchcock stopped me.

"I think we'd be best served to keep this conversation constructive, gentlemen."

I settled back in my chair, willing to let the inappropriate thoughts go for now.

"This isn't going to work, Owen," Fitzgerald mumbled to the lieutenant.

"Calm down, Robert. It will."

My frustration finally boiled over. "So have we

finally come to the part where you tell me why I'm here?"

Hitchcock nodded. "As I said before, we need your help."

"I got that. But what exactly do you need my help with?"

"We need your eyes," Fitzgerald said.

Afraid of how I might react to the bureaucrat, I looked to Hitchcock for clarification.

"Those rumors of rogue recruitment that Mr. Fitzgerald referred to? Not only are they true, but the practice may be much more widespread than we realize. Exactly how high up the food chain it goes we still aren't sure. But we believe it's an issue that affects multiple units within the department, from patrol to narcotics to homicide."

I cringed when I heard the word homicide. "I know every man and woman in that unit, lieutenant. And I can vouch for every single one of them."

"Unfortunately, we can't," Fitzgerald said bluntly.

"I don't know what you're implying, but I think you'd—"

"I'm sorry Scott, but he's right."

"Okay, so the department is filled with dirty cops. Do you think I'm one of them?"

"Absolutely not," Hitchcock said emphatically.

"Then what the hell am I supposed to do about it?"

"Help us find the ones who are."

For the first time in a long time, I found myself speechless. I knew there was a reason to be nervous about this meeting, but never in a million years would I have imagined this. My first instinct was to walk out of the office without saying another word, but I was too staggered to move. Hitchcock took my inaction as his cue to continue.

"I know how this sounds."

"I don't think you do."

"Trust me, I do. What I need you to do is at least hear me out before you come to any conclusions. Can you please do that?"

"I'm all ears," I answered, wondering if the lack of conviction in my voice was as apparent to the lieutenant as it was to me.

"The truth is there that isn't anyone in this entire department, let alone the homicide unit, that I trust more than you. You care about the job, you care about the men and women in that squad room like they're your family, and you care about that shield hanging around your neck and what it represents. Right now, it doesn't represent anything positive to a lot of people, and that bugs the hell out of you. You think about it when you're on the job, you think about it when you go home. You come in here blurry-eyed because it keeps you up at night. Am I wrong about any of this so far?"

My silent stare was all the confirmation he needed.

"I didn't think so. I know this because it does the same thing to me. But guess what? Not everyone in that squad room feels the same way we do. It doesn't mean they're bad cops. Most of them have never even considered walking outside the bounds. But they know about the ones who have, and they turn a blind eye to it. They see exactly what's going wrong out there and they don't do anything about it. You're one of the few who wants to make it better."

"And this is your opportunity to do that," Fitzgerald added.

Why the bureaucrat even felt the need to be here, let alone speak, was beyond my ability to comprehend, but voicing my confusion wouldn't help the situation, so I acted like he wasn't there. "You know as well as I do what happens to rats," I said to Hitchcock.

"No one is asking you to be a rat."

"Then what would you call it?"

"Doing your part to make sure this department doesn't drown."

The lieutenant's words played like a canned halftime speech, and so far, I wasn't motivated.

"Is this your melodramatic way of offering me a position in Internal Affairs? Because if you are, I'm afraid I'll have to decline."

"IA has no stake in this investigation," Fitzgerald declared."

"I was asking him," I shot back, pointing at my boss.

Hitchcock sighed. "Just like he said, Scott. This isn't a matter for Internal Affairs."

"Why not? These kinds of cases are the only reason those idiots even exist."

"Because we suspect that the crisis extends to that unit as well."

"Now we're calling this a *crisis*?"

"That's exactly what it is," Fitzgerald snapped back in what I could only assume was his tough-guy voice. "If you don't see it as such, then perhaps you don't have your finger on the pulse of things around here to the extent that your boss thinks you do."

My hand involuntarily curled up as I finally turned to the bureaucrat with my full attention. "Since you insist on putting your two cents into this conversation at every turn, why don't you tell me what the AG's stake is in this investigation?"

Fitzgerald was silent as he leaned back in his chair.

"At this stage, he's here as an independent observer. Nothing more," Hitchcock offered.

I kept my eyes on Fitzgerald, not believing a word the lieutenant had just said. "Nothing more?"

"This investigation is a DPD matter," Hitchcock reiterated. "My only concern is in making sure the right people are taking part in the investigation."

"Given the fact that we're having this conversation, I'm assuming you consider me the right people."

"Absolutely," Hitchcock affirmed.

"And have you approached anyone else about this?"

"Only you."

"Do you plan on approaching anyone else?"

Hitchcock looked at the bureaucrat for a long beat before answering. "Only if you decline."

I could already sense there was a lot more they weren't telling me. "So, if I accept this assignment, I'd essentially be a task force of one."

"The fewer people involved, the better," Fitzgerald insisted.

The full gravity of the conversation was finally starting to sink in, and I suddenly found it difficult to breathe. "I'm a homicide detective. Isn't this a tad above my pay-grade?"

"Yes, it is. And that's why you were the perfect person to approach," Fitzgerald said. "You're among the most trusted and respected members of the department. No one would ever see you coming."

"And you don't see anything wrong with asking me to betray that trust?"

"We're not asking you to betray anything," Hitchcock maintained.

"You're asking me to betray everything. You know as well as I do that if my participation in a corruption investigation of fellow officers ever got out, I'd be black-balled for the rest of my life. There wouldn't be another department in the entire country that would so much as sniff me."

For the first time, I saw something in the lieutenant's

narrow blue eyes that looked like hesitation. "It'll never come to that."

"How can you be sure?"

"Because you aren't actually investigating anyone. We are. All you're doing is collecting intel that can be used to assist us."

"Most of the guys out there would consider that being a rat."

Hitchcock leaned in close. "In here, we'd consider it essential to ridding our department of internal elements that could destroy it."

"Again, with the dramatics," I said with a sarcasm designed to mask my mounting concern.

"There's nothing dramatic about it, Scott."

"Okay, so are you going to tell me what this internal element is?"

"No."

"Why not?"

"Because you haven't accepted."

I sat back in my chair as a thousand thoughts simultaneously raced through my head. I couldn't grasp onto a single one. "So what's the first thing that happens if I accept?"

Fitzgerald answered. "We fully brief you."

"And how much time would I have to consider it?"

"Not a lot," Hitchcock said.

"I need something."

"Fine. Twenty-four hours. That means we'll reconvene here tomorrow morning at," he glanced at his watch, "Nine-thirty."

The room fell silent. Hitchcock and Fitzgerald were apparently waiting for my reply, but I didn't have one to offer them. As much as I tried to make sense of what they were telling me, the fact of the matter was that it made no sense.

For as good as it was that Hitchcock trusted me, there were dozens of trustworthy men and women in the unit. As far as I was concerned, nothing I'd accomplished in my three years as a homicide detective stood out as being head and shoulders above anyone else. There were no official commendations, no merit or leadership awards. I've never considered myself to be anything more than a hardworking, hard-nosed cop who did his best to uphold the Priest lineage of hardworking, hard-nosed cops.

I tried to imagine my father sitting in this seat having this conversation. He wouldn't have lasted two minutes before he either stormed out of Hitchcock's office on his own or was led out in handcuffs. Either way, he wouldn't have even entertained this bullshit, let alone taken part in it. The fact that I was still sitting here only confirmed something I'd known since I joined the academy nine years ago: I wasn't made of nearly the same stuff as my father.

"I guess I shouldn't bother to ask what's in it for me," I said to no one in particular.

Fitzgerald responded. "You shouldn't because the answer right now would be nothing."

Hitchcock shot him a fiery look. "You'd have the gratitude of a lot of important people, not the least of which are the citizens of this city," the lieutenant replied, apparently feeling the need to atone for Fitzgerald's blatant rudeness.

"In all honesty, you're the only person in charge whose gratitude actually means anything."

If the sentiment touched the lieutenant, he didn't show it. "I need you to keep something in mind over these next twenty-four hours, Scott. And I can't stress the importance of this enough."

"I'm listening."

28

"This decision is yours to make and yours alone. Don't discuss the details of this meeting with anyone, and that includes Detective Kimball. Is that understood?"

"It's not like I'd have any time with the Alvarez case playing out like it is."

"You mean Marisol Alvarez, the hotel maid?" Fitzgerald asked.

I turned to him with mild surprise. "How do you know about it?"

"Her name was published on the Mile-High Dispatch website this morning."

I pounded a hard fist against the arm of the chair. "Damn it."

"Take a breath, Scott," Hitchcock demanded.

"We haven't been able to talk to the victim's family yet. I guess those assholes at the Dispatch decided to do it for us. Will somebody please shut them down already?"

Hitchcock wasn't moved by my plea. "Should we pull you off the case while you make your decision?"

I couldn't help but glare at him. "I think I can handle it."

Hitchcock and Fitzgerald exchanged a glance. After a moment of silent deliberation, Fitzgerald nodded.

"Okay," Hitchcock said to me. "But I still want you to give this decision the appropriate attention."

"I will," I replied as confidently as I could, though the resolve in my voice was no stronger now than when the meeting started.

"Great. If you don't have any other questions, you're free to get back to it."

"I do have one question."

"Okay."

"What is it that I'm supposed to be observing? And

how do I know when I've observed something that's worth reporting back?"

Hitchcock and the bureaucrat looked at each other, something they only seemed to do when they were met with a question they weren't prepared to answer.

"That'll be fully addressed during your briefing," Fitzgerald finally said.

"Do you have any other questions?" Hitchcock offered.

If I thought the lieutenant would be even the slightest bit forthcoming in his responses, I'd have a million questions. As it stood now, I only wanted to get back to my real job. "I'm good."

With that, Fitzgerald promptly stood up. "Thank you for your time, Detective Priest," he said as he extended his hand.

I stared at it for a long time before extending my own. "When the lieutenant asks me to show up, I show up."

"Let's hope that's really true."

Overwhelmed by inappropriate thoughts that I desperately wanted to give voice to, I could only look at Hitchcock and nod as I walked out of his office. The lieutenant acknowledged me with a pat on the back that said, *thank you for not knocking the weasel on his ass.*

The nauseous feeling that came over me before the meeting had returned by the time I made it back to my desk.

Before this morning, the course of my day as a DPD homicide detective had been easily chartable. Recent events made the path a little more treacherous to maneuver, but I always knew where it would ultimately lead.

Once I left Lieutenant Hitchcock's office, it was as if all the familiar guideposts had disappeared, with nothing left behind to steer me in the right direction. I suddenly didn't know my place here. Would my days now be spent solving murders or observing my colleagues? Was I working for the citizens of Denver or the Attorney General's office? Most importantly, why hadn't I walked out of Hitchcock's meeting the moment the word *rat* entered the conversation? I had yet to come up with a definitive answer for that one. What I did know was that I was already regretting the decision. How deep that regret would ultimately go remained to be seen.

For now, I had to maintain my focus, guideposts, or no guideposts.

When I sat down at my desk, a sticky-note attached to the lamp caught my attention. I picked it up and immediately recognized Kimball's handwriting.

'Wrote up the initial case file on Alvarez. Pretty thin, but it's a start. I left it on your desk.'

I turned my attention to a desk that was entirely too cluttered and searched for the file. The fact that he said it was thin let me know that nothing new had broken since I left the scene. Aside from pools of the hotel attendant's blood in nearly every corner of the suite, we had nothing else to go on. This was one of those cases that would get tougher before it got easier, and it would require my full attention if I had any hope of solving it. It wasn't a good time to make career-altering decisions.

I'd made a mental note to see the department shrink about a possible hoarding disorder as I rifled through manila folder after manila folder in search of a case file that was clearly not on my desk. Overwhelmed by frustration, I was giving serious thought to sweeping the entire contents of my desktop into the recycle bin when the sound of a familiar voice stopped me.

"Looking for this?"

I turned around to see Kimball standing over my shoulder, the Alvarez file in hand.

"I've been looking all over for that."

He snatched it back as I reached for it. "You were in the lieutenant's office for so long that I was about to head back to the scene without you."

"And do what? You couldn't navigate your way through a McDonald's drive-thru without me, let alone a crime scene."

Kimball smiled as he dropped the file on my desk. "You spend half an hour in there, and you come out thinking you're Harry goddamn Bosch."

"Somebody's got to do the detecting around here."

"Well let's get going, Mr. Detector. We're already behind schedule."

"Sorry boss. It wasn't exactly my fault," I insisted as I rose to my feet.

Kimball walked up to me. Even at a solid six-one, two hundred and five pounds, I felt undersized next to his six-foot-four-inch massive frame of pure muscle. Kimball played strong-side linebacker for the Colorado State Rams for two years before a hip pointer prematurely ended his career. Seventeen years after his last game, he still had a physique that most twenty-year-olds would envy, and the cast-iron toughness to go with it.

"Of course, it wasn't your fault." he hissed. He kept approaching until we were practically touching.

"What the hell are you doing?" I said as I nudged him out of my personal space.

"Checking to make sure the time with the lieutenant didn't leave any brown spots on your nose."

I was irritated by the implication but knew I couldn't show it. "I'm only interested if it can be the same shade of brown as yours."

"You mean this chocolate mocha smoothness?" he mused as he stroked his clean-shaven cheek. "Not possible, my friend."

"Some guys get all the breaks."

"You get plenty of breaks."

"Oh yeah? Name one."

Kimball dug into his pocket and pulled out a set of car keys. "You get to drive."

I snatched the keys out of his hand. "You're generous to a fault."

"Says my ex-wife, every month after she cashes the alimony check."

I laughed; something I desperately needed to do. Then I led the way past Hitchcock's closed door and out of the squad room, hoping like hell that I'd find the guidepost I was still searching for. I hadn't so far, despite the presence of my best friend in the department. And I was becoming increasingly certain that I'd never find it again.

"Come on, Detective Kimball. Let's go solve this thing."

Kimball patted me on the back as we made our way to the elevator. "Nobody in the world I'd rather roll with."

I smiled despite the suffocating knot that was forming in my throat.

This was going to be a long twenty-four hours.

CHAPTER 4

When we arrived back at the Alvarez scene, we were greeted by half a dozen crime scene techs, an army of uniforms patrolling every floor of the hotel, and the backup team from homicide.

Detectives Jim Parsons and Alan Krieger were two of the best minds in the unit; a fact that they wouldn't hesitate to remind you of if you ever dared to forget. They were also two of the most cantankerous bastards on the planet. A combined fifty-two years of daily homicide work can do that to a couple. Krieger was the first to approach us. The snarky expression that had come to define his time-weathered face was on full display.

"Nice to know the leads finally found time to show up," he said before yelling over his shoulder to his partner. "Hey Jimmy, the guests of honor have arrived. Go into the hallway and tell the boys they can officially roll out the red carpet."

I responded by giving Krieger the finger.

"Love you too, Baywatch," Krieger countered.

I could only shake my head. A few months into the job, I was interviewing witnesses in a hit-and-run case when a woman walked up to me and made the random comment that I looked like one of the lifeguards from the TV show *Baywatch*. Kimball was the first to give me the moniker, and it stuck. Krieger was the only one who still used it, and he only did it to get under my skin. It worked every time.

"Don't bust on him too hard, Al. Our boy was busy enjoying the rarified air of Hitchcock's office," Kimball said.

Thanks for selling me out partner, was what I thought as I stared him down.

"No kidding?" Parsons chimed in as he shuffled toward the group. Unlike his counterpart, whose daily P90X routine kept him as fit as a man half his age, Jim Parsons looked every bit his sixty-one years plus a few. His high blood pressure and Type-2 diabetes did nothing to quell a Snickers habit that currently topped out at three per day, and I've had to scold him more than once about not keeping up with his doctor's appointments. But there wasn't anyone in the entire unit aside from Nathan whose work I respected more – present ribbing notwithstanding. "You weren't invited, Nate?"

Kimball frowned. "I never get invited to meetings with the big dogs, Jimmy. You know that."

"The Man still holding you down, eh Nate?" Krieger asked with his trademark smirk. "Aren't there programs in place to prevent that kind of thing?"

"As usual your lame-ass sarcasm adds nothing to the conversation," Kimball countered with a smirk of his own. "But if you can find a program that would make Hitchcock not act like such a prick every moment of the day, please let me know about it."

"Me too," Parsons added as he fished around inside his jacket pocket, no doubt hoping to catch a stray candy bar.

Krieger turned back to me. "So how were you lucky

enough to earn an audience with his royal majesty?"

I kept my poker face tight. "He wanted to swap stories about the wife and kids, discuss plans for the weekend, compare spring gardening tips. Usual nonsense."

"Aside from the fact that you don't have a wife or kids, you're a social hermit, and you wouldn't know a spring garden from a beer garden, I'm sure it was a great conversation."

Krieger and Parsons laughed at Kimball's quip like it was the funniest damn thing they'd ever heard. I joined in the laughter, hoping it would help push the conversation in a different direction. It didn't.

"You must've earned a big shiny gold star somewhere along the way, Scott," Krieger hissed. "The only time I ever got called into the lieutenant's office for a solo visit was when that cache of AK's went missing in evidence. To this day I think the SOB believes I took them."

"That's because he knows all about your apocalypse-prepping nonsense," Parsons chided.

"*Zombie* apocalypse-prepping to be exact. And it isn't nonsense."

I cut off Parsons' asinine response before he even had the chance to think it up. "Can we at least pretend that we're interested in doing our jobs here?"

Krieger's brow furrowed. "We've done our jobs already. And because you Sallys were late, we did yours too."

"Then, by all means, fill us in."

Krieger hit me with a cold look before turning to Kimball. "Hotel security is combing through surveillance tapes as we speak. As you already know, the cameras on this floor and the three floors below were offline last night, so all they have is the elevator, lobby, and parking garage footage. So far, the victim hasn't turned up in any. Obviously, neither has the perp."

Parsons took over where his partner left off. "And I just finished a rather heated conversation with Natalie Glassman, the hotel general manager. She was hot off a plane from LA, and she wasn't happy."

I felt my face flush with embarrassment. The purpose of coming back this morning was to interview Ms. Glassman. The only thing worse than dropping the ball is having your backup scoop it up and score. "How did that go?" was all I could manage.

"Heated," was all that Parsons could manage.

"Let's just say she didn't agree with our assessment that the entire hotel should be treated as a crime scene," Krieger added.

"Does she really think that the hotel can just return to business as usual after what happened here?" Kimball asked.

"That's exactly what she thinks," Parsons answered. "You'd figure all she'd want to talk about is her dead employee. Instead, she spends the entire time complaining that the patrol presence is scaring the guests. I told her the guests should be scared, and she should be too. She wasn't as inspired by that as I'd hoped she would be."

"So what are the chances we can actually shut the hotel down?" Kimball inquired.

"Logistically it wouldn't be easy," Parsons replied. "People would have to scramble to make different accommodations, and with that big tech convention in town, I'm sure every other room in the city is booked."

"The longer people are allowed to come and go as they please, the more our potential for finding evidence is compromised," I snapped back.

Krieger's eyes narrowed. "Tell that to Ms. Glassman.

Oh wait, you were supposed to do that already."

"I've already apologized for being late. What else am I supposed to—"

Krieger cut me off. "You were handling important business, Scott. We get it. But the next time you choose to shoot the breeze with Hitchcock instead of working your crime scene, all we ask is that you don't do it on our time."

"Chill out, Alan."

Kimball's terse directive was enough to get Krieger to back down. At that point, I decided that the next directive would come from me, and it wouldn't be near as diplomatic.

Kimball continued. "Unfortunately, we can't force the hotel to shut down completely, so we have to focus on what we can control. Where are we at with interviews?"

"We've talked to just about everyone who could offer anything useful," Parsons said. "Patrol has been going door-to-door for about an hour. So far it hasn't produced any meaningful noise."

"I suppose everyone heard about the Mile-High Dispatch leak?" I asked the group.

"What else is new with that piece of garbage?" Krieger muttered.

"Any idea how they got her name?" Kimball asked.

"Probably one of the first responders looking for a quick dollar," I speculated.

The snarky glint in Krieger's eye returned. "Are you suggesting that someone connected to this investigation is on the take?"

"I'm not suggesting that anyone is on the take, Alan. Don't put words in my mouth."

Krieger put his hands up in mock surrender. "Easy, kid. I was just joking around. What's with the sensitivity?"

I needed to take a deep breath before responding. "Who's sensitive?"

"Right now, I'd say the entire department is," Kimball answered. "But this isn't the time for a group therapy session to explore our feelings about it. Has Marisol's family been given a formal notification?"

Parsons nodded. "Her oldest daughter was contacted an hour ago. A patrol unit has already paid a visit."

"We should follow up," Kimball suggested.

I agreed. "Do we have an address for her?"

"I'm assuming you can get it from the hotel's HR office," Parsons said.

I looked at Kimball. "I'll send one of the uniforms for it."

"As long as you don't mind making the trip to see the Alvarez kid by yourself," Kimball responded. "I could do without the grieving family piece this morning."

In two years as his partner, I'd never known Kimball to be comfortable with the grieving family piece, especially when children were involved. In one of the rare moments of vulnerability I managed to pry out of him, he confessed that the grief over the disintegration of his own family was mostly to blame.

When I first met Kimball, I could always count on Monday morning stories about his fun-filled weekend visits with his two boys Jordan and Tyler. Over time, the stories became less frequent, until one Monday morning when he showed up to work with the court-approved petition by his ex-wife to move his sons halfway across the country. The boys had come to visit four times since the move. Those visits were the best times of his life, he'd say. Until it was time for them to leave. "*It feels like dying every time,*" was how he described those tear-filled moments of saying goodbye. It's a feeling he says he relives after every meeting with a victim's family.

"No worries. I got it covered," I said with a pat on his shoulder.

"Great. Now that that's settled, what are we going to do about this no witnesses, no suspects, no murder weapon issue we seem to have?" Krieger asked.

"We'll keep checking in with hotel security regarding the surveillance footage. Beyond that, we make sure that every single person who was in the hotel last night is interviewed and we keep reiterating to hotel management the importance of keeping a lid on the extra-curricular activity," I answered. "It might be impossible to close them down completely, but we can at least get them to monitor the traffic flow a little more closely. Aside from that, we trust everybody else to do their jobs and wait for the break that we all know is coming."

Parsons smiled. "Spoken like a true lead detective. For a while, Alan and I were starting to think you didn't want the job."

"I swear Jimmy if you say one more thing about us being late..."

Parsons laughed so hard his distended belly shook. Unfortunately, his partner wasn't so jovial.

"Hey kid, next private meeting you have with the lieutenant, make sure you vouch for me regarding those AK's. Maybe if he had a trusted ear to vet my character, he'd finally stop shooting me dirty looks."

Despite his open smile, I couldn't tell if Krieger was joking or not. I was leaning toward not. "I don't know what makes you think I'm such a trusted ear, but whatever."

Krieger shrugged. "Call it a healthy distrust of the brass. Don't mind me."

"I'm doing my best not to."

"On that note, why don't we break up this little sewing circle and try our hands at some police work," Kimball said.

"I haven't heard a better idea all morning," I declared as I made my way toward the front door. The relentless browbeating about my time in Hitchcock's office was starting to wear thin, and even though I was sure I'd maintained adequate composure, I had no confidence in my ability to keep it together for much longer.

Kimball met me in the hallway, followed by Krieger and Parsons. Krieger, as usual, was the first to speak.

"I'm on my way to meet up with hotel security to see if there's any progress on that footage. Jimmy is going to catch up with some of the uniforms to see how the door-to-doors are coming."

"Then I'll take another crack at Natalie Glassman," Parsons said with a subtle smile.

"Just make sure you don't hold back the Parsons charm this time, huh big guy? Kimball joked.

"Yeah, Jimmy. Bat those luscious eyelashes of yours a few times," I added for good measure.

Parsons' pale face turned beet red. "I'll see what I can do."

"We'll catch up with you guys at HQ," I continued. "Hopefully, there will be some decent notes to compare by then."

"Hope so," Krieger said. "And good luck with Marisol's family."

It was the first time I'd detected sincerity in his voice. "Thanks."

"You got it. And as far as all the Lieutenant Hitchcock stuff, that's just me busting your balls a little bit. I personally don't trust the guy as far as I can throw him.

There aren't many of us who do after what's been happening lately. You're still fairly new around here, so you haven't been burned the way some of us have. Nobody wants to see that happen."

Even in his apology, Krieger was still pressing. I tried to remain nonchalant as I responded. "Thanks for the concern, but it wasn't a big deal. He only called me in for a quick progress report on Alvarez."

"Without the other lead detective?" Krieger asked as he pointed at Kimball.

"I told you, Alan, I don't get invited to the meetings with the big dogs."

"Hell, I'll file the EEOC paperwork for you, brother."

Krieger and Kimball shared a laugh. I would've joined in had I not already known that the laughter was at my expense. "I have a family to talk to. I'll see you guys later."

Kimball and I made our way to the elevators while Krieger and Parsons lingered in the doorway of the suite.

"Remember kid, I'm just busting your balls," Krieger yelled as I stepped on to the elevator.

I un-holstered my middle finger and was preparing to fire in response, but the elevator door closed before I could.

"Crotchety old bastard," Kimball sniffed as he pressed the lobby button. "Don't let him get to you."

Too late, I thought as I stared straight ahead, wondering how I was going to tell Kimball that he'd also gotten to me.

"There's just a lot of unnecessary paranoia floating around the unit right now, and the brass, including Hitchcock, is largely to blame for it," Kimball continued. "If they would show some actual leadership and sit down openly with us for ten minutes that would probably be the end of it. But because they choose not to tell us anything, we assume they're hiding stuff. Obviously, our time on the street has conditioned us to think the worst about most situations. Makes us all more hypersensitive than we should be. I think Krieger's got it worse than most."

"And where do you fall on that spectrum, Nate? Are you hypersensitive too?"

"Not about your meeting with Hitchcock." Kimball cracked a smile. "But I am curious."

We stepped off the elevator into a lobby that was mostly empty except for a front desk clerk and two uniforms standing near the entrance. We waited in silence as one of the officers made the trip to the Human Resources office for Marisol's address. I didn't speak again until we were settled in the car.

"Hitchcock and I weren't talking about Alvarez, by the way. I would never discuss a case in-depth without you being there."

Kimball nodded his understanding, but his silent stare indicated that he was still searching for an answer, so I gave him one.

"We were actually talking about my father."

The explanation had apparently been satisfactory as Kimball promptly redirected his attention out the window. After a prolonged silence, he asked, "How is he?"

I started the car and pulled out of the docking bay where we'd parked. The Tuesday morning traffic was more annoying than usual. "He seemed like himself, thorny disposition and all. That's what's really throwing me about this whole thing."

I cursed myself as I forced down the lump that had infiltrated my throat. I had no business using my father as a cover story, mainly because I couldn't seem to talk about him these days without something inside of me cracking, but it was the best excuse I could come up with.

"I've heard the onset of Alzheimer's symptoms can be really tricky to predict," Kimball replied in the firm tone he used when he needed to temper his emotion. He looked up to my father almost as much as I did, even visiting him a few times while he was still able to live at home with my mother. Kimball walked out of the last visit with the same look on his face that he had right now.

I would definitely burn in hell for this one. Still, it was better than the alternative that the truth provided.

We fell back into silence for much of the trip back to HQ. Kimball complained about the pile of statements he would spend the rest of the morning logging, but that was the extent of the conversation. I tried to keep my mind focused on Marisol Alvarez's family and the hope that speaking to them would offer at least some insight into a murder victim that we currently knew nothing about.

But my thoughts kept drifting to Hitchcock and his sidekick from the AG's office. As much as Krieger's insinuations irritated me, I understood his distrust of the lieutenant, now more than ever. I didn't believe for a second that he would be completely forthright in his intentions, even if I did agree to help him. Just like I didn't believe for a second that Robert Fitzgerald was in that meeting only as a passive observer.

Kimball may have bought the cover about my father, but it did nothing to change the reality of the meeting, and the thermonuclear fallout that would most likely result. If I were being honest, I'd admit that Krieger was one hundred percent right to question me. Without realizing it, I'd already betrayed him, Kimball, and every other hypersensitive member of the force, simply by not telling Fitzgerald to fuck off the moment I learned who he was. That betrayal would be something I'd have to live with at least until tomorrow morning's meeting.

I could only hope to summon the will to do the right thing by then, even though I still had no real sense of what the right thing was.

CHAPTER 5

Marisol Alvarez's children didn't learn about her murder through the Mile-High Dispatch leak as I had feared. They instead got the news via a phone call from the Four Seasons management. Not that it mattered. There's no ideal way to receive the news of a loved one's sudden, violent death.

By the time I arrived at the tiny Northwest Denver apartment that Marisol shared with her two daughters, the shock and despair of the initial news had given way to detached numbness.

The thirteen and sixteen-year-old sisters sat quietly on the couch, arms tightly interlocked as if their collective existence depended on the physical contact. They were surrounded by aunts and uncles, cousins and friends, but no one could seem to penetrate the force field of protection that the sisters had built around themselves. I'd had a difficult time penetrating that force field myself, as my ten-minute visit had thus far yielded little more than a chorus of angry demands from the other family members that I find whoever was responsible and do it quickly. This was followed by the standard *"I'll do whatever I can"* response that every detective is obligated to give in such a situation. My assurances were met with a silence that I could only interpret as disbelief. The reaction was one I'd grown quite accustomed to in recent weeks.

Choosing to ignore the rest of the room, I moved my chair close enough to the girls so that only they could hear me. "I'll find the person who did this to your mother. You have my word."

Christina, the younger of the two, was the first to look at me, her damp eyes sending pleas that her voice couldn't. I smiled and offered a nod of reassurance as her older sister finally summoned the will to speak.

"How exactly do you plan to do that?" Dana Alvarez asked pointedly. "Do you even have a suspect?" The maturity in her voice betrayed her young age. She would need every bit of that maturity going forward.

"Not yet. We're doing the absolute best we can, but we could use some help."

"With what?" Christina asked in a voice that didn't possess nearly the measure of her sister's.

"We need to learn as much about your mom as possible: who her friends were, any romantic relationships she may have had, what her state of mind was prior to yesterday. Things like that."

The blank stares that I got back indicated the need for a more straightforward approach.

"Did you notice anything strange about her behavior over the past few days? Was she worried about anything? More quiet than usual?"

"It was just the opposite," Dana offered as she dabbed at her eyes with a tissue. "She was really excited about her new job. All she could talk about was how nice the hotel was and how much more money she'd be making. It was the happiest I've seen her in a long time."

"Did she talk about anyone she worked with?"

"No one specifically. She said she was part of a crew of four that was assigned to clean the bigger rooms."

"Any problems with the crew?"

"No. Like I said, she seemed really happy." Dana paused. "Much happier than the last place she worked."

"And where was that?"

Dana and Christina exchanged a glance. Christina tightened her grip on her older sister's arm.

"She was a housekeeper."

"For whom?" I asked as I pulled out a notepad that desperately needed to be filled in.

"A cop."

I immediately stopped writing. "Say that again?"

"The man whose house our mom worked in. He's a police officer in your department."

I almost asked Dana to repeat herself again, but I knew her response wouldn't be any different the third time around. So I swallowed hard and asked the question I knew I needed to ask.

"What's his name?"

Dana looked at her sister as if she needed confirmation to answer the question. When Christina nodded her approval, Dana turned back to me. "Oliver Brandt."

I nearly dropped my notepad. Thankfully, neither of the girls seemed to notice. "And how long was she employed by him?"

"Three years. And she mostly worked for his wife," Dana clarified.

The distinction between Oliver Brandt and his wife Bethany made sense. The former is a commander of the DPD SWAT team and one of the higher-ups rumored to be at the center of the department's brewing corruption scandal. The latter is a wealthy real estate developer whose fingerprints are all over the Denver skyline. Only one of them would have the financial resources to hire a full-time housekeeper, and it wasn't the one who was still fifteen years away from collecting his meager pension. Still, any connection to Commander Brandt, no matter how loose, would bring scrutiny to the case that no one wanted.

"Why did she leave?"

Dana's face stiffened. "She was fired."

"On what grounds?"

"On the grounds that Oliver Brandt is a sexist, racist piece of shit."

Christina's eyes grew wide with embarrassment as she pushed her sister's arm. "Dana!"

"What? I'm sorry, but it's true." She turned to me with eyes that were now dark with anger. "He didn't like my mom from the beginning, like she had no business being in his house or something. She would always overhear conversations between him and Mrs. Brandt. He'd say stuff like, "*is she even legal*?" Mom just ignored it and did her job, the same as she always did. But it never stopped bothering her."

I nodded and allowed her to continue.

"Mrs. Brandt was nice though. She liked having these huge parties for all of her important friends. Mom always looked forward to those because she got paid extra. A couple of weeks before she was fired, she came home all excited because she was going to work some big to-do that Mrs. Brandt was having for the mayor. Mrs. Brandt took those parties pretty seriously. So did mom. She said she came away from them knowing more about political and business deals than they would ever tell you on the news. Everybody called her CNN because she loved to report back on everything."

Dana smiled. It was a pretty smile, and I wondered if she'd inherited any parts of it from her mother. The thought made me sad, and I pushed it aside as quickly as I could.

"So Oliver Brandt was the one responsible for firing your mother?"

"That's right. She never told us the whole story, but she told us enough. He wasn't a good person."

The adrenaline spike I suddenly felt made it difficult to keep the pen in my hand steady, and I had to put it down. "What did she tell you?"

"Mrs. Brandt was out of town the day mom got fired. Apparently, Mr. Brandt came home while she was there cleaning, and something happened. There was a big fight, and Mr. Brandt got angry. Mom got angry too, and he told her to leave and never come back. I never saw her more upset. She was shaking the entire night." Dana paused. "She was scared too."

I looked at Christina. It was clear the recollection was upsetting her.

"Did she tell you why?" I asked Dana.

"I begged her to tell me what happened, but she wouldn't. After a while, I finally stopped asking, but I knew that whatever happened between them hadn't stopped bothering her. Even with the relief she felt at getting a new job, she wasn't the same after that night. He did something to her. I don't know what, but it was bad."

A feeling of dread came over me as I picked up the pen and wrote Commander Brandt's name in my notepad. I couldn't bring myself to write anything more.

"Did he do this to her?" Christina abruptly asked.

"Do what?"

"Kill her?"

The question was startling, but I maintained my composure. "Commander Brandt didn't kill your mom."

"Would you tell us if you thought he did?" Dana countered with a hard glare.

"I know him, Dana. He isn't responsible for this."

50

"How can you be so sure?"

I wasn't, but I couldn't tell her that. "As I said before, I'll find the person who actually did this. I promise."

At that moment, I looked up to see that the rest of the eyes in the room were on me. Some of the stares were angry like Dana's, some were desperate like her sister's; all were demanding an immediate response to a problem they now thought I was helping to perpetuate. I hadn't told Dana the truth when I claimed to know Oliver Brandt. The truth was that I hadn't spoken a single word to the commander in my nine years on the force, but I refused to give in to the notion that a member of my department was capable of something as heinous as what happened to Marisol Alvarez, corruption scandal or no corruption scandal. It was apparent that Dana had already made up her mind, however, and her conviction was enough to sway her family. Soon, the rest of the community would be swayed too, and in their minds, I'd be reduced to nothing more than another crooked cop trying to cover it all up.

As I looked at the faces surrounding me, it was clear that I'd lost the room, and it would only get worse the longer I stayed. So I gave Dana my card, along with the request to call should she need to.

After assurances from her aunt and uncle that the girls would be properly looked after, I left; much further away from square one than when I'd arrived.

I sat in the car for what felt like a long time, staring at the only five words that I'd managed to write down during the brief interview: *Marisol Alvarez/ Commander Oliver Brandt.* But it wasn't the words I'd written that filled me with the angst that currently rendered me immobile, it was the thought of the words I needed to write next: *connection... lead... potential suspect.* Due diligence required that I write those words, even if I didn't want to believe them. Due diligence would also require me to follow up with appropriate action.

Hence the angst.

My current state didn't allow for a rational plan through which to carry out that action. Kimball would obviously be the first person I'd involve, but Kimball is former SWAT, meaning that his history with Brandt is extensive. I'd have to tread carefully when I presented the news, and trust that whatever his personal reaction was, he'd be on board with the depth of investigation that would be required. With the way this day was going so far, I wasn't sure if I could trust anything.

Add one more screwed up thing to this already royally screwed up day.

When I looked up from my notepad and out the car window, I quickly realized that another item was about to be added to that ever-growing list.

CHAPTER 6

I'd just taken a long pull from a bottle of water that had been baking in the car for at least a week when I saw someone attempting to enter the apartment building I'd just left. A double take confirmed the identity of the person I was seeing, though my disbelief at seeing her refused to subside.

I jumped out of the car without thinking as Kyle McKenna stood impatiently at the front stoop. She was pressing apartment buzzers indiscriminately in the hopes that someone would let her in. Typical of her bottom-feeder tabloid journalist methodology.

I held my badge out in front of me as I approached, wishing she would give me an actual reason to arrest her. Unfortunately, there was nothing in the penal code that outlawed her lack of professional integrity.

Her already bright face lit up even more when she saw me coming. Not exactly the reaction I was hoping to inspire.

"Well, if it isn't Scott Priest and his waving-the-badge routine. It's time to up your game, my friend. That stopped scaring me a long time ago."

"I saw you trolling through here and figured you'd obviously gotten lost. I decided to be a nice guy and offer you an official police escort back to wherever it is you came from. This isn't the safest neighborhood for pretty young vultures."

"What a charmer. You must've been the stud of your alternative high school."

"Believe me, when it comes to you, the charm is forced."

"Of course it is," she said with a broad smile that communicated her disbelief.

Kyle was attractive even when she wasn't trying to be – which by my estimation was most of the time. Her curly auburn hair was usually pinned back in some haphazard ponytail, a messy-chic that she probably saw in some magazine. Her wannabe hippie vibe was usually completed with a pair of faded blue jeans, a tee shirt from her 1990's concert-going days, and a pair of open-toed sandals that never took a season off, including the dead of winter. Her sharp green eyes were always probing, and if you allowed her the opportunity, they would look deeper into you than you'd ever want a pair of eyes to go. It was a trait that most good journalists had. And Kyle McKenna was a good journalist. Unfortunately, she chose to align her skills with one of the worst tabloid rags in the country, a rag that devoted most of its ink to skewering the Denver PD and the men and women who served in it. That made her the enemy.

"If you've finished putting the moves on me could you please put the badge away? I would hate for the neighbors to think that I'm being harassed."

I smirked as I hung the shield around my neck. "Seems to me you have the market cornered on harassment, Ms. McKenna. The fact that you leaked Marisol's name this morning..."

"That wasn't me."

"Really? And I suppose its pure coincidence that

you're stalking her children right now. Do you think I'm that stupid?"

"Your lack of intelligence, though well-documented, has nothing to do with the current situation, detective. Marisol has been formally identified, which now makes this a full-fledged news story. It also makes Dana and Christina fair game."

"There's nothing fair about your game, Kyle. They just lost their mother for Christ's sake."

"And I'm very curious to know why. I thought you would be too."

"Our motivations are couldn't be more different."

When an elderly woman emerged from the apartment building, Kyle took it upon herself to hold the door open for her. I would've thought it a nice gesture had I not known what she planned to do after the woman cleared the doorway.

"I'm not finished talking to you," I declared before she could take her first step inside.

"You mean you're not finished insulting my character."

"Wouldn't you actually need character before I could insult it?"

She sighed as she held on to the door. "Don't you have a murder to solve?"

When she attempted to walk through the door, I pushed it closed in front of her.

"That was totally unnecessary."

"You published Marisol's name before her family could be notified. Did you even care if her kids saw it?"

Kyle's smooth sun-soaked face suddenly hardened. "I told you I didn't have anything to do with that."

"It doesn't matter. I can't let them be exploited any more than they've already been."

"Look, I know the DPD is in this cute little

totalitarian phase right now, but this is still a free country with a free press. I don't need your permission to do anything." With that, she began pushing apartment buzzers again.

"They might be too busy grieving to answer the door."

"No shit they're grieving. I'm not a total goon."

"You're trying to interview them for a newspaper article in the midst of the worst time of their lives. I'd say that makes you a goon."

Kyle rolled her eyes. "You just interviewed them. What does that make you?"

"A homicide detective doing my job."

"I'm doing my job too."

"I've seen first-hand what can happen when you do your job."

"What's with all this hostility? It's not like I've ever written about you. Sure you're a butthole, but you're also a solid cop. As far as I'm concerned, that's all my readers need to know."

I was less than overwhelmed by her flattery. "What about all the other solid cops in the department? Why not expose your readers to them?"

"Because the bad ones sell papers. And from what I'm starting to learn, there are a lot more of them than there are of you."

"The mud-slinging has officially begun," I responded through clenched teeth. "How have you not been sued for libel by now?"

"Because in spite of all their self-serving press conferences and hollow proclamations to the public, your bosses know that everything I write about is true."

Despite my lack of tolerance for Kyle and the newspaper she wrote for, there were plenty of people within the department who were afraid of her, and after this morning's meeting with Hitchcock, I was finally beginning to understand why.

Her first investigative piece on the DPD came on the heels of Mayor Sonya Richmond's U.S. Senate campaign and subsequent victory last November. A few weeks before the election, Mayor Richmond's husband and campaign manager Elliott had become the target of a series of searing accusations made by a former FBI agent. It was believed that he not only attempted to rig the election but that he also arranged for the murder of a colleague and lawyer named Julia Leeds when she threatened to expose him. According to former Special Agent Camille Grisham, Elliott's extramarital affair with Julia also played into his motivation.

Even though the story was as convoluted as any the city had ever seen, among members of the department it would have added up to little more than another sordid sex scandal involving power and politics – two things the average cop cares nothing about. But when two homicide detectives were shot while working the Leeds murder, the story took on an entirely new dimension.

The man believed to be responsible for those shootings was a patrol officer who infiltrated the department under an assumed identity. Shortly after he confessed to killing Detective Walter Graham and severely injuring his partner Chloe Sullivan, he also hinted at playing a role in Julia Leeds's death, though he refused to say what that role was. What he did say was that he didn't act alone, claiming that his co-conspirators were high-level officials. After more than two and a half months in jail awaiting trial, Joseph Solomon has yet to reveal anything more.

Many in the media assumed that these high-level officials were somehow associated with the department.

Once Kyle McKenna began her daily in-depth reporting on the story, assumption became fact in the minds of the public, and as more layers were peeled away, including the possibility that Solomon may have had a direct connection to Elliott Richmond and possibly the mayor, the figureheads within the department began to panic.

The result was an informal code of silence that precluded them from addressing the story in public or even amongst themselves. The code of silence eventually extended into every corner of the department, much to the dismay of officials from the AG's office who were assigned the case. This practice allowed members of the media – the Mile-High Dispatch especially – to run wild. Every article written by Kyle featured the latest report of police brutality, racial profiling, and every other transgression that a cop could be accused of. And she rode the wave of negativity all the way to record circulation. She did her share of good reporting along the way, but she also succeeded in throwing a lot of good people under the bus.

I'd managed to evade the wrath of her pen up to this point, despite being quoted by her more than a dozen times over the past two years, but I figured it would only be a matter of time before I made the honor roll. Perhaps the task that Hitchcock charged me with would finally be enough to clinch my spot.

"If there are so many dirty cops flooding the street, why aren't you out there chasing them down?"

"Because the story I need to cover exists right here," Kyle answered as she impatiently pressed another apartment buzzer.

"The only thing that exists here are two very vulnerable, very frightened teenage girls who miss their mother. Since you wouldn't recognize a human-interest story if it punched you in the face, I don't see what angle you could possibly be working."

"I'm working the Marisol Alvarez is connected to Oliver Brandt angle."

My poker face must not have been strong enough because Kyle seemed to sense my surprise immediately.

"Tell me I'm not scooping you, detective," she said with a thin smile.

My expression tightened. "Wouldn't you just love that? Sadly for you, I'm already well aware of the connection."

"How well aware are you?" She was starting to get that probing journalist look in her eye that I dreaded.

"Marisol worked for him."

"In what capacity?"

"I figured you would've already known that."

"I do. I just want to see how much you know."

My eyes lit up with a sudden realization. "Has this whole thing been your passive-aggressive way of pinning me down for another interview?"

"*Pinning* you down for an interview? Who's being passive-aggressive now?"

I smiled in spite of myself. "You wish."

"Can you please just answer my original question, detective?" A soft, almost vulnerable expression flashed across her face that I found very appealing – and I hated myself for it.

"Off the record, of course."

"Of course."

"Marisol worked in Commander Brandt's home for three years. Something happened, and she was let go."

"And?"

I shrugged. "You claimed to know so much about it, I was hoping you could fill in the rest."

She looked disappointed that the ball had landed

back in her court so abruptly, but true to form, she quickly picked it up and ran. "Marisol and your commander were the only two people in the house during the altercation that led to her firing, so most of what I've gathered is second-hand information. But it's fascinating second-hand information."

"Fascinating, huh? You've certainly got my attention."

"According to someone who was apparently very close to the situation, Marisol was fired because she overheard a telephone conversation that she shouldn't have."

"What was the nature of the call?"

"She wouldn't tell him. When he asked again, she said that he was better off not knowing, so he didn't press."

"Go on."

"Marisol did explain that she accidentally walked into Brandt's office while he was in the midst of this conversation. When she saw him, she immediately walked back out. But based on what she'd heard and Brandt's panic at seeing her, it was a conversation she wanted to hear more of. So she stood outside the office while the conversation continued. According to my guy, Marisol was quite the hoarder of information."

"Where I come from, it's called being too damn nosey for your own good."

"That's certainly another way to put it."

My flippant remark aside, the story seemed to be in line with what Dana Alvarez had told me about her mother's inquisitive nature.

Kyle continued. "Marisol stood by the door listening for over five minutes before Brandt suddenly walked out. When he saw her standing there, he immediately accused her of eavesdropping. She denied it. Some kind of back and forth ensued – mostly yelling on Brandt's part. Next thing you know, Marisol is out of a job."

"It sounds to me like there was more to this than mere eavesdropping. Maybe there had been some prior issues with Marisol, and Brandt simply viewed this incident as the final straw."

"As far as I've heard, Bethany Brandt loved her. If there were prior issues with Marisol's performance, they were Oliver Brandt's issues alone."

I made a mental note to put Bethany Brandt on my interview list. Convincing her to actually sit down for that interview would be another story. "Could your source tell you anything else?"

"Only that Marisol seemed different afterward. She was certainly upset about being fired, but he suspected there was more to it."

The same suspicion that Marisol's daughters had. "Did he offer up any theories?"

Kyle shook her head. "Marisol was tight-lipped until the end."

"Do *you* have any theories?"

The sudden gleam in her eye was blinding. "Of course I do. That's why I'm here."

"Why don't you give the Alvarez girls a break and run your theories by me instead?"

"For the same reason I've never run any of my theories regarding the DPD by you."

"Try me."

Kyle was silent for a moment as if she were seriously considering the request. Then she shook her head. "Compared to our usual run-ins, this conversation has been civil, dare I say pleasant. If it's all the same, I'd rather keep it that way."

"Pleasant might be a stretch."

"Okay, tolerable."

"That's more like it."

After an extended silence that bordered on uncomfortable, Kyle turned her attention back to the apartment buzzers that she'd already thoroughly worked over. She raised a finger to press Marisol's apartment again but quickly thought better of it. "If no one has answered by now they're probably not going to. I keep pushing my luck and someone is bound to call a cop."

"And I sure as hell won't vouch for you."

The soft edges returned to Kyle's face as she walked away. "You're a jerk."

"I do what I can," was my reply as I tipped an invisible cap to her. "Just make sure you keep me in the loop if any of your theories actually start to pan out."

She looked back at me with a smirk. "I think I'll call Detective Kimball instead. I always thought he was the cuter one anyway."

Ouch. I placed a hand on my chest as a phantom pain pierced my heart. "I'll be sure to tell him."

The tires on Kyle's daisy yellow Volkswagen Bug screeched as she drove away.

Making the short walk to my own car, I shook my head to clear the cobwebs. This simple little condolence visit to the Alvarez girls had become much more than I'd bargained for. Now that I knew that multiple people were openly discussing Brandt's name in connection with a murder victim, the pressure to investigate him only intensified, as did my concern that the process would require more than the few simple questions that I had hoped to get away with. I always did my best to avoid complications, both in my professional and personal life. Oliver Brandt was becoming a major complication.

As I approached the car, I spotted a DPD patrol

cruiser slowly headed in my direction. I waved it down, assuming the officers were conducting a drive-by of Marisol's apartment or stopping by for additional follow-up. The cruiser slowed to a crawl as it came upon me, but it didn't stop. Instead, the officers inside responded to my second wave with two of the sharpest glares that I'd ever been on the receiving end of. The young patrol men held their icy looks for the duration of their drive past. My arm dropped as they disappeared around the corner.

It was possibly the strangest exchange I'd ever had with fellow officers, and one of the most unnerving. I stood by my car for over five minutes in the hopes that they would return with the logical explanation that I deserved.

They never came back. Neither did my hope that this would turn out to be anything less than the shittiest day of my life.

I started the car with the serious thought of tracking down the boys in the cruiser for a harsh lecture on the value of professional courtesy, but the phone call from Kimball diverted my attention.

"Say something to make me smile," I demanded as I answered the call.

"You look beautiful today."

"Try again."

"We just got a hit on the surveillance footage."

I blew out a sigh of relief. "Now we're talking. How significant?"

"Alan is bringing a copy of the tape back to HQ as we speak, so we'll find out together."

"I'll be right in. Should I stop for popcorn on the way?"

"White cheddar. And a box of Junior Mints."

My smile lasted the entire drive back to HQ.

Nothing can turn around a shitty day quite like solving a homicide.

CHAPTER 7

Kimball, Krieger and I were huddled around Parson's computer as he inserted the USB disk that contained the hotel surveillance footage. I shifted impatiently as the technology-challenged Parsons attempted several times to open the file before his partner finally took the reins.

"This footage will end up on Unsolved Mysteries by the time you're finished dicking around with it," Krieger snapped as he opened the file with two mouse clicks.

"You know Unsolved Mysteries hasn't been on for like ten years, right?" Kimball informed him.

Parsons glanced over his shoulder with a smirk. "Einstein over here still thinks we're in the twentieth century."

"So do your computer skills," Krieger shot back.

"Silence is golden, boys," I said as the first grainy images appeared on the monitor. "Tell us what we're looking at, Jimmy."

Parsons turned his attention to the screen. "This was taken from the parking garage adjacent to the hotel last night at approximately 8:33 P.M., three hours before the victim's estimated time of death. Keep an eye on the Honda."

Almost on cue, a white Honda Accord appeared in the camera's view, coming to a stop in a parking spot near the stairwell. A tall, slender man quickly emerged from the driver's seat.

"Who's that?" Kimball asked.

"His name is Arturo Sandoval," Krieger answered. "He's been identified as an employee of the Four Seasons, part of the overnight maintenance crew."

"Ok, so why are we looking at him?" I asked with an impatient sigh.

Krieger waited a few seconds before answering. "Because of her." He pointed to the screen as a woman exited the passenger's side door.

"Is that?"

Parsons nodded. "It most certainly is."

"Marisol Alvarez," Kimball muttered. "Outstanding."

"But wait. It gets much, much better."

Arturo met Marisol on the passenger's side of the car where the two briefly embraced. As Marisol tried to cut the exchange short, Arturo pulled her back into him, kissing her with a degree of force that clearly made her uncomfortable. He staggered backward as she nudged him away. There was a short exchange, nothing heated. Then Marisol disappeared into the stairwell. Arturo, dressed in a light-colored windbreaker, blue jeans, and a Colorado Rockies baseball hat, lingered by the car for a few seconds before following her.

"So they were lovers," Kimball surmised.

"None of the staff we spoke to has made that connection," Parsons replied. "But the tape doesn't lie."

Just like my dad predicted.

"Was Arturo interviewed?" I asked as I watched him enter the stairwell.

"No," Krieger confirmed. "He wasn't scheduled to work last night. We only interviewed employees who were on duty at the time."

"Marisol wasn't due to start work until four o'clock

the next morning. What would she be doing with him so soon before her shift?" I asked.

"Maybe she got her start times mixed up," Kimball speculated. "According to the log, she'd been on the night crew for the first week she was here. She could've simply been coming to work on autopilot. Graveyard shifts can do that to you."

"Which means that Arturo may have only been giving her a ride," I added.

"We'd considered that too," Parsons said as he fast-forwarded through static footage. "Until we saw this."

When Parsons pressed play, the scene had shifted from the parking garage to the hallway of the presidential suite. The time stamp on the bottom of the screen read 8:41 P.M.

"I thought the cameras on that floor weren't picking anything up," a wide-eyed Kimball said.

"They weren't," Krieger answered. "Beginning at 8:58. They were working just fine before that. For some bizarre reason, the security guys didn't go back that far until we asked them to."

Unlike the brief but intimate scene that played out in the parking garage, the dynamic between the couple was tense as they stood outside of the suite. The muted audio didn't allow us to hear their words, but their exaggerated hand gestures and rigid body language more than adequately told the story.

The four of us watched in silence as an agitated Marisol slipped a key card into the door of the suite. Arturo hovered behind her. With each second that passed, the timbre of his voice appeared to rise.

Kimball shook his head as he looked at me. "This is almost too easy."

I nodded in agreement and turned back to the screen, just in time to see Arturo enter the suite behind

Marisol.

Parsons stopped the video at that point. "And there it is kiddos. The closest thing to a smoking gun that we're probably gonna get."

"Any footage of the good Mr. Sandoval leaving the suite?" Kimball asked with a loud sigh.

Krieger shook his head. "The camera malfunction occurred while he was still inside."

"Lucky bastard," Kimball hissed.

"I'd say his luck just ran out," Parsons countered.

I agreed, but I couldn't shake the image of Marisol long enough to respond. In homicide, we aren't often afforded the opportunity to see a victim in action hours before their death. Most of the time we have to use our imaginations to fill in the details that a photo couldn't provide: the way they walked, the way they talked, the manner in which they dressed. Sometimes those details were accurate. Most times, they weren't. In Marisol's case, the details were crystal-clear – from the pressed neatness of her long ponytail to the way her hotel uniform hung loosely around her shapely body to the way she kept her arms in tight to her sides as she walked. The only thing left to the imagination was her voice, and how it must've sounded when she uttered her first cry for help.

"It's time to pay Mr. Sandoval a visit," I said as the sound of Dana Alvarez's mature but vulnerable voice echoed in my head.

Parsons groaned as he stood up from the computer. "Figured you'd say that. I already put in a call to the Four Seasons HR office." He handed me a Post-It note with what I assumed was Arturo's address on it.

Kimball smiled from ear to ear. The chase was his favorite part. "You ready to saddle up, partner?"

I put a hand to my holstered Glock. "Let's ride."

"Can't storm the Alamo without the cavalry," Krieger said as he put on his jacket. "Besides, my hefty partner here is the quickest draw in the West."

Parsons pointed his half-eaten Snickers in our direction and fired. "And I never miss."

With that, the Four Horsemen rode off into battle, no one bothering to warn Parsons about the long strand of caramel dangling from his chin.

CHAPTER 8

Even though we were reasonably confident that Arturo was the guy, we decided against bringing along a patrol presence. The initial contact with a potential suspect always worked better when you appeared to come in peace. As far as he'd know, we were merely interviewing hotel staffers who were not on duty last night, and his name was next on the list.

I usually did the talking in such instances, born diplomat that I am. Kimball gave no indication that this instance would be any different.

"If I'm lucky, I'll be able to save the news about the surveillance footage until after we get him downtown," I said to the group as we approached Arturo's apartment building. "Unless the sight of you three beauties sends him scrambling out the back exit."

"Do you want me to swing around in case he does?" Kimball asked, still ready for the chase.

"Let's just play it cool for now," I advised. "You never know, he could turn out to be a real sweetheart."

I buzzed apartment 504. After a few moments, a gruff voice came over the intercom.

"Yeah?"

"Arturo Sandoval?"

The delayed response told me this was going to be a

problem visit.

"Mr. Sandoval?" I repeated.

"Who's this?"

"Denver police department, sir. We understand you're employed at the Four Seasons hotel. We're in the process of gathering witness statements and would like to ask you some questions about an incident that occurred there last night." I looked back at the cavalry. They seemed satisfied with my level of tact.

Based on the silence I was receiving from the other side of the intercom, Arturo wasn't so impressed.

"Mr. Sandoval?" I buzzed his apartment again. No answer. I looked at Kimball. He nodded.

"I'll go around."

The ex-collegiate linebacker ambled around the side of the building with near effortless speed.

Parsons and Krieger tensed, both of them instinctively bringing up their hands near their shoulder holsters.

"Are we going in?" I asked as my finger hovered over the buzzer marked MANAGER.

They nodded simultaneously.

Seconds later, a female voice came over the intercom. "Manager's unit."

"Denver police. There's a tenant in your building that we'd like to speak to and he won't answer his door. Arturo Sandoval in 504."

Her irritated sigh indicated this was an all-too-common occurrence. "Come in."

The sound of Kimball's booming voice captured my attention before I could walk inside. "Denver P.D.! Stop right there!"

Shit.

The adrenaline spike carried me off the front stoop and around the side of the building before I realized I'd even taken my first step.

"Cover the inside," I yelled back at Krieger and Parsons as the pair raced through the front door.

I heard the first explosion as I rounded the corner. A second explosion quickly followed. I arrived at the rear of the building to the distant sound of screeching tires and the sight of a slumped-shouldered Kimball holding his service pistol. My mind naturally gravitated to the worst-case scenario.

"Are you hit?"

"No," Kimball hissed as he stared down the empty alley. "The asshole gave it his best try though."

I had difficulty gathering my breath in spite of the short distance I'd run. "Did you catch the make and plate of the car he got into?"

"The car was a late model Dodge Durango. I couldn't read the plate."

"What the hell happened?"

Kimball holstered his Glock. "Apparently he high-tailed it down here the instant we ID'd ourselves because he was already out the back door when I arrived. I told him who I was, ordered him to stop, and that's when he pulled out the hand cannon."

".357 from the sound of the pop."

"Had to be. I was too busy ducking to get a clear beat on it. He took a second shot, and by the time I got to my piece he was in the car."

"It would've been easier for him to come out and tell us that he was Marisol's killer."

"No joke," Kimball said with a light chuckle.

A noise from the back door quickly put us both back on edge.

"Everything okay out here?"

"We're fine," I assured Krieger as he and Parsons stepped through the door. "He took a couple of shots at

Nate before he jumped in his car."

"Do we have a beat on him?" a breathless Parsons asked.

Kimball took out his cell phone. "Black Durango is the best I can do. I'm calling it in now."

While Kimball stepped aside to make the call, I made my way into the apartment building. "We'll get some units out here to keep watch on the place and hopefully track down the SUV. In the meantime, let's have a chat with the apartment manager."

CHAPTER 9

"I'd love to say that he was one of those quiet tenants who mostly kept to himself, paid the rent on time, and helped the little old ladies with their groceries. But that would be a hearty crock of shit." Melinda Abrams, the manager of the Woodland Oak apartment complex, clearly wasn't prone to mincing words when it came to Arturo Sandoval. "He paid his rent on time for the most part. But beyond that, he's been nothing but a thorn in my side."

"So this isn't the first run-in he's had with cops around here?" I asked.

"Lord, no. Between him, his degenerate meth-head friends, and his poo-butt girlfriends, there'd be a cop on the premises at least once every couple of months."

"Violence?"

"Disturbing the peace type stuff, loud music waking up the neighbors, yelling that lasted for hours, but never anything that kept him locked up. What do you guys want him for?"

I looked at Kimball. He didn't hesitate to answer.

"Information in connection to a murder investigation. Oh, and for shooting at me."

Melinda's brittle, pale skin lost another shade. "You mean he actually killed someone?"

"We're trying to figure that out," I answered.

Her eyes widened with intrigue. "Fuckin' A, that's crazy. Who was it?"

I resisted the urge to roll my eyes as I pulled out my notepad. "Right now, we have to focus on finding him. Anything you can tell us about his background would be helpful. Family, close friends, references from his apartment application. Anything."

Melinda bit down on her chapped lower lip as she searched her memory. "I don't know the names of any of the losers he hung out with. He doesn't have any family, at least none that he's ever talked about. And the application process around here is kinda loose so there wouldn't be any references."

Kimball's irritation was starting to bubble. "So as far as what you know about the guy, he might as well be a ghost."

"All that we're required to have on file is our tenant's habitation status and job information. The other details don't really concern us."

The group collectively sighed at the dead-end we realized was ahead of us.

"Sandoval was employed at the Four Seasons as a night maintenance worker," Parsons said with a huff. "That's the one thing we do know about him."

"The Four Seasons?" Melinda asked with a quizzical look. "For how long?"

"Not long," Parsons reported.

"Well ain't that a step up. I'm shocked that he passed the background check."

"A step up?" Kimball asked. "Where did he work before?"

"The last job I had listed for him was as a groundskeeper for one of the richies in Cherry Hills Village."

This news had barely registered as a blip on the group's radar screen. For me, it was like a punch in the stomach.

"Do you happen to have the name of this Cherry Hills richie?" I asked Melinda with a forced composure.

"Not off the top of my head. I can grab the file though."

"That won't be necessary," Kimball insisted.

"Indulge me, Nate," I said.

Melinda put her hands on her bony hips. "So am I getting it or not?"

Kimball shrugged. "I guess you are."

I didn't say anything until Melinda returned, afraid that if I revealed any aspect of my theory, it would compel me to explain the whole thing. Fortunately, no one asked.

Melinda was reading the paper as she walked back into the room. "Oliver and Bethany Brandt are the people he worked for. 78244 Ridgeway Road. I have their phone number too if you need it."

The group remained silent, compelled now more by shock than bored indifference.

"I'd love a copy of that file if you can manage it," I said.

"I have photocopies in the drawer, so you can have this one," Melinda said as she handed me the page.

I nodded my thanks and gave her my card with the instruction to call the police if she had even the slightest suspicion that Arturo might return. She seemed downright exhilarated by the prospect.

"I'll help in whatever way I can, detectives. 'Bout time somebody locks that psycho up."

With that, the cavalry followed me single-file out of the building. No one said a word.

CHAPTER 10

An all-points-bulletin immediately went out for Arturo Sandoval and his black Dodge Durango, with a still image from the hotel surveillance tape and a previous mug shot going out to media outlets across the state. According to the official police statement, Arturo was a person of interest in the Marisol Alvarez homicide. According to Detective Nathan Kimball, he was the man who tried to render his two sons fatherless. For that, there would most certainly be hell to pay.

Aside from an open box of .357 Mag rounds, a search of Arturo's apartment turned up nothing useful. There were no pictures or other correspondence that would have indicated a connection to Marisol. No sign of the clothes he was wearing on camera the night before. No bloodstained knife soaking in the kitchen sink.

Uniform patrols would continue scouring the area on the off-chance Arturo would be stupid enough to come back. I knew he wouldn't be that stupid, which meant our best chance would be the five-thousand-dollar carrot we were dangling from the crime-stoppers tip line. A payday like that meant that the backstabbers were already sharpening their knives.

Krieger and Parsons made their way back to HQ while I stuck around the apartment complex, waiting for

Kimball to fill out the incident report on his run-in with Arturo. I knew what the conversation was going to be once he finished, yet the time spent imagining it did nothing to prepare me for what I'd actually say.

The fact that Arturo had worked for Brandt was significant. For starters, it created another solid connection between him and Marisol. But it also pulled Commander Brandt that much deeper into the investigation. Given his apparent disdain for the household help, he'd most likely never spoken a word to Arturo that didn't involve an opinion on the way his grass was cut, but that wouldn't matter one bit, especially to the media sharks like Kyle McKenna. At best, she'd find a way to turn this story into yet another unfair black-eye for the department. At worst...

I wasn't willing to go there quite yet.

As Kimball approached, it was obvious that his aggravation with the day's turn of events had yet to subside. "Can we get the hell out of here already?"

"Way ahead of you, my man."

I held my breath for the entire walk to the car.

*****

"You knew that Arturo worked for Commander Brandt, didn't you?" Kimball asked as he choked the steering wheel.

"Yes."

"May I ask how you knew?"

"Marisol's daughters."

Kimball looked at me with confused eyes. "What would they know about it?"

"During the interview, they revealed that their mom worked as Brandt's housekeeper. More specifically, his wife's housekeeper. After I learned this, I did a quick search for the Brandt residence and came up with a Cherry Hills Village address. The same one Melinda Abrams just gave us. It didn't take a degree in astrophysics to put it together from there."

"And when were you planning on telling me all this?"

"There really wasn't any time before now." That was technically true, but I would've found any excuse possible to put off the conversation.

Kimball tightened his grip on the wheel. "Well ain't this a kick in the head."

"And we haven't even dealt with the worst part yet."

"Which is?"

"The Alvarez girls despised Brandt, to the point that they suspected he had something to do with their mother's murder."

"Tell me you didn't entertain that nonsense."

"Of course I didn't, but the perception is out there, and not just with Marisol's daughters. After I finished with them, I ran into Kyle McKenna. She didn't come right out and say it, but she's definitely barking up the same tree."

"She's always barking up some tree," Kimball sniffed. "Who gives a damn what she thinks?"

"More people than we want to admit to, which is why we have to be proactive about this."

"Meaning?"

Here it was. The part I dreaded. "I'd like to start by talking to Mrs. Brandt."

Kimball's grunt was about as loud as I expected it would be.

"I'm not happy about it either," I said. "But we have to clear the bases on this, if for no other reason than to spare her the possibility of being ambushed by some reporter without the first clue of what's going on."

"Why not just brief the commander and call it good?"

"We can do that too, but Bethany Brandt is the one who actually had the working relationship with Marisol. The same was probably true with Arturo. She could speak better to the kind of people they were, and what relationship, if any, they may have had. If this thing plays out the way we think it will, the Brandt's are going to be a part of the story anyway. All we're doing is getting a sense of how big that part will be."

Kimball was quiet for a long time before responding. "This is some murky territory, Scott."

"You have a history with Commander Brandt, so I get that you want to walk this rope carefully. If you'd prefer that I visit Mrs. Brandt alone..."

"It's not that."

I stared at him in anticipation of a response that he was hesitant to give. "What is it then?"

"You know IA has been riding his ass about Chloe and Walter, right?"

"I've heard the rumbles."

"Yeah, well, it's more than rumbles. Rumor is they have records that prove the commander was on the phone with Walter the moment he was shot. There's also a statement from Chloe saying she witnessed Walter in a heated exchange with Brandt outside the commander's office less than an hour before. That statement has been sealed, and Chloe hasn't been willing to talk about it."

I sniffed loudly, a nervous tick I've had since I was a kid. I was familiar with the accusations the same as everyone else in the department. And like everyone else I wanted nothing more than to dismiss them. Then I had a meeting with Lieutenant Hitchcock and a representative from the Attorney General's office, and suddenly I couldn't dismiss anything.

"What's your point?"

"My point is its all bullshit. He and Detective Graham go back twenty-five years, yet people are trying to say that the commander is covering up something in connection to his murder. It's ridiculous to the point of being laughable, but it's not stopping them. What do you think they're going to do when they learn that he's connected not only to Marisol Alvarez but also to the man who's the prime suspect in her murder?"

"I could give two shits about what the idiots in IA do."

Kimball's brow furrowed. "Some of us can't afford to be that nonchalant about it."

"So what do you suggest?"

"I think we have to circle the wagons around Brandt."

"By doing what?"

"Burying the Alvarez connection."

I winced at the pain as my heart began a slow descent into my stomach. "You're joking, right?"

"No, I'm not."

"Nate, that's completely unnecessary. The chances of the connection being anything beyond business are slim to nonexistent. If we start burying stuff that doesn't need to be buried, then we're asking for trouble. But if we can get out in front of this thing by addressing it before anyone else does, the story dies the natural death that it's supposed to."

"You obviously don't know how internal investigations work around here," Kimball replied in a dismissive tone that I didn't appreciate.

"Apparently you do. So educate me."

The skin in Kimball's jaw bulged before he took a deep breath to settle himself. "No need to get heated. We obviously want the same thing."

"You sure about that?" I asked; still feeling rather heated.

We stopped at a red light just in time for Kimball to look me square in the eye. "Yeah, I'm sure."

"Then you won't have any problem paying Bethany Brandt a visit."

Kimball held my eye contact as the light turned green. I could only hope we were looking upon each other as the allies that we'd always been.

"Fine, let's go."

CHAPTER 11

Mindful that an unannounced visit by a homicide detective was the worst nightmare of any cop's family, I called the downtown offices of *Brandt Architecture and Design* ahead of our trip. We promptly changed course upon learning that Bethany Brandt was spending the day working out of her Cherry Hills home office.

"You think they'll pat us down before letting us through the gates?" I asked in a vain attempt to cut the tension that had settled over us.

A half-smile briefly infiltrated Kimball's face. "I've heard the country-clubbers have a real problem with you sandy-blond types, so I'd say it's a good possibility."

I chuckled with relief at the reappearance of the Kimball that I knew and loved. I couldn't understand where the paranoia over Brandt and Internal Affairs was coming from. Of everyone I knew on the force, Kimball was usually the last one to be weighed down with the politics of the department. He hated spending time at HQ almost as much as I did and hated rubbing shoulders with the brass even more. From where I stood, Brandt was part of the brass, and protecting them wasn't in my job description. I'd assumed it wasn't in Kimball's either.

Then again, the list of things I was wrong about only

seemed to grow as the day went on.

Entry into the Brandt's gated community wasn't nearly as formidable as I'd speculated, though the gatekeeper – a middle-aged man in a blue polo shirt and crisply-pressed khakis – did have to check our names against a clipboard ledger before we were permitted inside.

"Just follow the signs and stay to the left, detectives. Mrs. Brandt is expecting you."

Her massive corner lot did not betray the excessive formalities that we had to endure for the mere privilege of laying eyes on it. The house itself looked like something out of the antebellum south, with its low-hanging magnolia trees, grand columns, and old-fashioned wrap-around porch. Kimball drove slowly up the veranda, parking his DPD Homicide-Edition Ford Taurus behind a cream-colored Cadillac Escalade.

I wasn't sure if it was the rarified air of my surroundings or the fact that I was about to have a personal and very uncomfortable conversation with a woman I'd never met, but I suddenly didn't want to be here.

"Hey, don't go getting all wet in the diapers," Kimball chided, obviously noticing my change in demeanor. "This was your bright idea."

"I'm fine," I insisted as I wrung my numb hands. "Let's just get this over with."

After all the talk of housekeepers and gardeners, I couldn't hide my surprise when Bethany Brandt answered her own door.

"You must be Detectives Kimball and Priest."

Kimball smiled politely and extended his hand. "That's right ma'am. I'm Nathan Kimball, this is Scott Priest."

Bethany's smile was equally polite as she shook our

hands. "Bethany Brandt. Normally the sight of two detectives at my front door would be cause for a great deal of concern. I appreciate you calling ahead."

"Of course, Mrs. Brandt. The last thing we wanted to do was alarm you."

"As I said, I appreciate it. Still, I'm assuming this isn't a social visit."

One glance was all it took to know that the woman was all business. Her wide brown eyes framed a soft, inviting face, with none of the aloof air that one generally associated with the super-rich. But the strength of her presence was overwhelming. Even dressed as she currently was in a soft-knit white blouse and dark-washed denim jeans, she could walk into any station of life anywhere in the world and take full command of it. She was as breathtaking as the lavish wealth surrounding her, and I knew that I had to gather myself quickly if I hoped to conduct anything approaching a professional interview.

"Unfortunately, it isn't," I said after I cleared my throat. "We'd like to ask you some questions about a woman who used to work for you."

Bethany's attractive face dropped. "I figured as much. I haven't been able to stop thinking about Marisol since I heard about her this morning. Please, come in."

We followed her through a marble-floored foyer into the home office.

"Can I offer you anything?" she asked as she reached into a mini-refrigerator that had been built into the wall next to a wet bar.

"No thank you," I answered, though Kimball and I probably had the same thought of regret at the sight of the Sam Adams Seasonal brew lining the shelves.

She took a long pull from an exotic-looking water bottle before sitting behind her desk. Kimball and I followed suit in adjoining armchairs.

"I couldn't go into work today," Bethany said in a tone laced with genuine sadness. "It's just too much to believe that something like this could happen to her. Marisol was honestly the sweetest person I've ever met. And she was the best mom too." Bethany covered her mouth to stifle a sudden gasp. "Dana and Christina. Those poor girls. Have they been notified?"

I nodded. "I paid them a visit earlier this morning."

"How are they holding up?"

"As bravely as two young teenagers can under the circumstances."

"I need to reach out to them as soon as possible."

"I'm sure that would be appreciated. They spoke very highly of you."

The strain in Bethany's face eased slightly. "I'm glad to hear that. I do miss them."

Kimball looked at me and rubbed his chin, the high sign to get the interview moving.

"They told me that the circumstances of their mother's departure from here were somewhat acrimonious."

Kimball promptly stopped rubbing his chin.

"Acrimony is a strong word," Bethany replied with a hint of discomfort.

"I use it only because they say her termination was abrupt and unexpected."

"It certainly wasn't anything I wanted."

"Can you expand upon that at all?" Kimball asked.

"Is my husband aware that you're here?"

Kimball and I glanced at each other before I turned back to Bethany.

"No, ma'am. This is a fluid investigation, and we're following up on the few leads we have as quickly as we can. There wasn't time to consult him. I hope that won't be a problem."

"It's not a problem at all, Detective Priest. I understand and appreciate your urgency. I'm only asking because if you want to get the full story of why Marisol is no longer employed here, you'll have to get it from him. I only have his version of events to draw from."

"And what is Commander Brandt's version of events?"

She blew out a deep, mournful breath before answering. "My husband claims that he came home one day unannounced and caught Marisol in our office going through his personal file cabinet."

Kimball looked to me for a follow-up question, but I couldn't come up with one. This was already differing wildly from what I'd previously known to be the truth.

"What's in this file cabinet?" Kimball finally asked.

"Financial records and personnel files related to the department. All confidential. He claims that he always kept it locked."

Kimball perked up noticeably. "Did she tell him why she was going through it? Could she have just been cleaning it and he mistook her intentions?"

"According to him, she couldn't offer a good reason for being there. He got angry, of course. She began arguing back; saying he had no business questioning her, and that was that. He fired her on the spot."

"Did you ever get the chance to clear things up with her?" I asked.

"I tried. I called her cell phone dozens of times. I even showed up at her apartment once. I could never reach her. She clearly wanted nothing to do with me."

"Do you think it was because she was guilty of what the commander had accused her of?" Kimball asked pointedly.

"In my heart of hearts, I don't think she was guilty of anything, but there's no possible way I can prove that. Especially now."

"Then why would he be so adamant in accusing her?" I retorted.

"As I said before, if you want the full story you'll have to ask him."

Kimball looked at me as if to say n*othing left to see here – move along.* But I wasn't quite ready.

"Based on what I gathered from the girls, you and Marisol were close, that last incident notwithstanding. Did she ever share things about her personal life?"

"Explain what you mean by personal."

"Did she ever talk about relationships? Specifically, about anyone she may have been dating?"

Bethany shifted in her chair, the first time I'd noticed any discomfort.

"Marisol was a young, attractive woman. I'm sure she had plenty of suitors. But she never talked about them to me. Yes, we were close, but there were certain things she was guarded about. I certainly understood that."

"So you never saw pictures or overheard her speak of male friends?"

"No."

From the corner of my eye, I saw Kimball giving me the high sign again. This time I ignored him.

"Do you know a man by the name of Arturo Sandoval?"

A second shift, this one much more pronounced than the first.

"Yes, I do. He was employed as our landscaper for seven months."

"Seven months? Isn't that a long cycle for a private landscaper in Colorado?"

"He did some maintenance work for us in the winter. This is a large property, detective; a lot for two incredibly busy people to keep up with on our own."

"Completely understandable," I replied in a contrite tone. "I'm just trying to get as complete a picture as I can."

Bethany nodded. "He found another job a few weeks ago, in the facilities department of the Four Seasons. The hotel called us for a reference. My husband gave a glowing recommendation."

"So he was a solid employee?"

"As far as I know. I didn't deal with him a lot." Her eyes were suddenly downcast at her feet.

"Was he employed here at the same time as Marisol?"

Bethany hesitated as if she had to think hard to make the connection. "The landscapers didn't spend much time in the house, so it's doubtful any of them would have met Marisol."

"Be that as it may, were they here at the same time?"

Kimball sighed just loud enough for me to hear. I continued ignoring him.

"Yes," she answered before taking a labored breath. "If you don't mind, why are you asking so many questions about Arturo Sandoval?"

Kimball opened his mouth to speak, but I cut him off before he could get the words out.

"Because he's emerged as the prime suspect in Marisol's murder and we're trying to establish as many connections between the two as we can. We've already established the fact that they worked together at the Four Seasons. We've established that they were together only a few of hours before she was killed and that he was most likely the last person to talk to her. And we've established that they were employed by you at roughly the same time. The only thing we haven't established is a possible motive. That's why it's necessary to ask you these questions, Mrs. Brandt."

The little remaining composure in Bethany's face completely gave out, and her eyes began to water. "My god, this is such a nightmare."

When she put her hands over her face and quietly began sobbing, Kimball shot me a look that would have killed a lesser man where he sat. I certainly felt bad that she was taking the news so hard, but I knew the questions were necessary. Apparently, my partner didn't feel the same way. Why was that?

I reached for a box of Kleenex on a nearby end-table and set it down in front of her. She kept a shaky hand over her eyes as she reached for a tissue.

"Thank you."

"You're welcome. I understand this is difficult and I'm sorry."

"It's okay. I know you have to ask the questions. It doesn't make them any easier to answer though."

"Of course not, Mrs. Brandt," Kimball said as he placed a comforting hand on her arm. "You've been very helpful under the circumstances."

She finally composed herself enough to lift her head. "I wish I could offer more."

"That's quite alright," Kimball assured her. "You've told us plenty."

Looking at her face, I wasn't so sure about that. "Just to clarify, you never saw anything from Mr. Sandoval that made you uncomfortable. No aggressive behavior, no moodiness, no off-color comments?"

"I didn't interact with him much, as I've said. But the interactions I did have with him weren't anything out of the ordinary." She punctuated her sentence with a loud sniff. Clearly, she and I shared the same nervous tick.

90

I smiled as I turned to Kimball. "Well, if you don't have anything else, I think we can wrap this up."

Bethany stood before Kimball could respond. "Thank you for coming, detectives."

I extended my hand. She was slow to accept it. "Thank you for taking the time out of what I know is a very busy, very stressful day."

"I second that, Mrs. Brandt. Your cooperation is very much appreciated."

She managed a gracious smile. "I couldn't have you two reporting back to my husband that I was a hostile witness, now could I?"

"You're far from it," I insisted.

Hostile? No. Not entirely truthful? Quite possibly.

We accepted the second offer of a cold water bottle on our way out, no doubt both wishing that we could take a cold bottle of beer instead.

CHAPTER 12

"So, did you get what you came for?" Kimball asked as we left the Utopian confines of Brandt's gated community.

"Not entirely. I think she was holding out on us."

"What makes you say that?"

"Did you see how uncomfortable she got when I brought up Arturo? She couldn't move the conversation away from him fast enough. And the reason she gave for Marisol's firing smells like total bullshit."

I could see a slow build of frustration coming over Kimball. "So now you're saying Mrs. Brandt was lying?"

"I don't think she was lying. I think she was repeating the same bullshit story that was told to her."

"So Commander Brandt was lying?"

"Unless she was part of some clandestine operation for DPD Internal Affairs, what business would a housekeeper have going through Commander Brandt's department personnel files? It makes zero sense."

"Ninety percent of what we see out here makes zero sense. But that doesn't change the reality of it."

"That may be the case most of the time, but in this instance, I have good reason to be skeptical."

"And what reason would that be?"

"Kyle McKenna."

Kimball's laugh was almost deafening. "So she's the great bastion of truth now? Give me a break, man."

My mind flashed back to the Dispatch leak of Marisol's name and all of Kyle's negative profiles of cops and her stalking of Marisol's daughters, and I suddenly felt embarrassed that I'd even brought up her name. But the information she'd provided felt too important to ignore. "She spoke to someone with an inside track on Brandt and Marisol's situation who told a much different story than Mrs. Brandt."

"How different?"

"According to this version, Marisol was cleaning the house and accidentally walked in on a phone conversation that the commander was having. Being the nosey sort that she was, she lingered outside the door and continued listening. Brandt caught her, laid into her a bit, then fired her."

"For lingering outside his office while he was on the phone? Doesn't that seem silly to you?"

"Of course it does. But like you said, just because something makes zero sense doesn't mean it's untrue."

"Okay. Suppose it is true. What reason would the commander have to lie about it? And if he is lying, why would his wife, someone who purportedly loved Marisol so much, support it?"

"Exactly, and now you know why I'm leaving here so unhappy."

Kimball sighed. "I know it's in your nature to try and find smoke where other people don't see it, but in this case, you really have to consider the source of your information. This is Kyle McKenna we're talking about. The only reason she even exists is to screw over every member of our department the first chance she gets. That includes you, Scott. We're interviewing Bethany Brandt based on some ridiculous theory that Kyle concocted, when the asshole who killed Marisol Alvarez, the asshole who took a shot at me, is still running free out there. Shouldn't we be putting our resources into him? I mean, does it even matter why Marisol was fired? She's dead. All that should matter to us is who killed her. And it sure as hell wasn't Commander Brandt."

I couldn't deny the logic of Kimball's argument, even if I couldn't completely reconcile it. Perhaps if he'd sat in on my meeting this morning, he'd be more sympathetic to my paranoid state.

And I would be the first to admit that I was becoming increasingly paranoid.

That paranoia made me wonder if Kimball was right. Perhaps I needed to keep my sights set on what was in front of me, on what was tangible. The video of Arturo outside the hotel suite with Marisol was tangible. The fact that he ran at the mere mention of our presence was tangible. The shot that he took at Kimball was tangible. Everything else was based on theory, and unless you're Sherlock Holmes, theories don't solve murders.

The drama with Commander Brandt and Marisol was my first good look inside the tall weeds that no doubt awaited me when I accepted Lieutenant Hitchcock's assignment. It was also my first indication that I wouldn't find anything good in there, no matter how much positive change I could affect; no matter how noble my intentions were.

There may have been something seriously wrong in the department, but I couldn't be the one to fix it.

In that instant, I'd finally found the guidepost I was looking for, and it came in the form of one word.

No.

That had to be my answer to Hitchcock.

No.

I never knew that such a simple word could have such a powerful effect.

No.

The weight of a thousand elephants was suddenly lifted from my shoulders.

I'm sorry, Lieutenant Hitchcock, but the answer is no.

The smile on my face was so broad that it physically hurt.

Find someone else to catch your rogue officers. And tell the bureaucrat to fuck off while you're at it.

Between my smile and the heavy hand I put on his knee, Kimball must've thought I'd suddenly lost my mind, or fallen in love with him.

"Something I should know about you, partner?"

I gave another firm squeeze for good measure before letting go. "No need to get excited down there, Nathan. It's just my way of telling you that you're right about this whole Commander Brandt thing. It's too easy to look for smoke where there isn't any. That's what the Kyle McKenna's of the world do. You and I catch killers. Arturo Sandoval is our killer. Simple."

Kimball blew out an exaggerated sigh of relief. "All I can say is thank god I don't have to get excited. That's when it gets awkward."

We shared a laugh, and it felt completely normal.

Unfortunately, it would turn out to be the last genuinely normal moment we'd share for a very long time.

CHAPTER 13

I hadn't even noticed the red and blue flashing lights until Kimball was in the process of pulling over.

"What the hell is this?" he said with a scowl as he eyed the rear-view mirror.

"I think we're getting lit up. What did you do now?"

The unmarked Crown Victoria followed as we pulled into a nearby parking lot. "Wrong place, wrong time. Story of my whole damn life."

I chuckled despite Kimball's obvious irritation. "Just let me do the talking, okay? I have a way with cops."

"Shut up."

I was still laughing as we stepped out of the car. It was strange for a fellow unit to get our attention this way rather than a call over the two-way, but I didn't think much of it as we approached the Crown Vic.

That changed when I saw who was behind the wheel.

"Good afternoon, detectives," a smiling Commander Brandt bellowed as he stepped out of the car.

Kimball and I had seemingly stopped on the exact same dime, both of us at an immediate loss for words.

"Always good to run into the DPD's finest, especially out here in the sticks," he mused as he continued his approach.

"Good to see you, commander," Kimball said as he went in for a handshake.

I kept a respectful distance.

"You too, Nathan. How's the cozy homicide life treating you?"

"I have to admit, I do miss the Kevlar sometimes. But the jacket and tie work most days."

"You wear it well," Brandt observed before turning his attention to me. "Detective Priest. I don't think we've officially met." He stuck out his catcher's mitt of a hand.

"Nice to officially meet," was all I could manage, and even that was a struggle.

He nodded and turned back to Kimball. "So my wife says you came out for a visit. Sorry I wasn't there to greet you. To what did we owe the pleasure?"

Talk about getting right to the point. I let out a nervous breath, thankful that the question hadn't been directed at me.

Kimball let out an equally nervous breath as he scrambled for a response. "A murder investigation."

"Marisol Alvarez?"

"That's right."

"I heard you had a beat on the potential perp, but he slipped away before you could collar him. Is it true he took a shot at you?"

Kimball nodded. "Thankfully he missed."

"Can you track him?"

"There's a BOLO out now. We have the make and model of his car plus photos. We'll catch him."

"And god help him when you do," Brandt said with a wink. "So, back to why you were at my house."

"Right. Well, it actually has to do with the guy who took a shot at me."

Brandt didn't flinch. "Really? How's that?"

Kimball's purposeful hesitation prompted me to step

in. "The man we're looking for is named Arturo Sandoval. We have surveillance footage of Mr. Sandoval entering the presidential suite of the Four Seasons with Marisol shortly before her body was discovered there. When we went to his apartment to question him, he fled out the back door, taking a shot at Nathan in the process. During our questioning of the apartment manager, we discovered a connection between Arturo and Marisol that went beyond their mutual employment at the Four Seasons."

"Which was?"

"They both worked for you."

The confusion on his face was less than convincing. "Arturo Sandoval, huh? I can't say that name rings a bell."

I wanted to pretend that I hadn't heard that. Unfortunately, I couldn't let it go. "The apartment manager had you listed as his last known employer."

"Bethany has employed a lot of people in a lot of capacities, so I suppose it's possible that he worked for us."

"Your wife said you provided a reference for him when he got his job at the Four Seasons. Apparently, you gave him a glowing recommendation." The words came out before I could stop them.

"Were those the specific words that Bethany used? Glowing recommendation?"

"It was something to that effect," a nervous Kimball cut in. "But there wasn't much to the meeting beyond that. We were mainly interested in tying up any loose ends that may have existed in the connection between Sandoval and the victim. We feel pretty confident that those loose ends are tied up now."

Brandt kept a skeptical eye on me. "Do you concur with that, Detective Priest?"

From the corner of my eye, I could see Kimball nearly rubbing the skin off his chin. "We won't know that for sure until we catch him."

The expression on Brandt's face brightened. "Nothing in the world I like better than a thorough cop. I guess the apple really doesn't fall far from the tree."

The commander's smile did little to ease my queasy stomach. I probably should've thought twice before challenging him, even if it was the instinctive thing to do. Brandt's initial reaction indicated that he'd recognized the challenge. His subsequent smile suggested that he was still figuring out how to respond.

The weeds just got a little bit taller.

"I'd actually been hoping for the chance to talk to you one day."

I immediately tensed. "Is that right?"

"Your old man was something of a mentor to me. I came up through narcotics when he was heading the unit. I'd call him a hell of a cop, but that wouldn't do Carl nearly enough justice."

The smile on my face wasn't entirely manufactured. "I appreciate that."

"Sorry to hear about what he's been going through. How's he been holding up?"

My smile promptly went away. "Some days are better than others."

"That Alzheimer's is a fucking beast. Bethany's dad is dealing with it too. Tears you apart to see them suffer that way."

"Yes, it does."

"It was bad enough what happened to your brother. A lot of us are still reeling over that one."

Unable to find a suitable word to respond with, I merely nodded.

"Your family has experienced more than its share of

knocks, but the tide has a way of turning. From what I hear, you're doing them both proud."

"Trying my best."

Kimball cleared his throat to break the subsequent silence that settled over the three of us. "In my completely biased opinion, there isn't a better detective in the entire department."

"I've heard the exact same thing," Brandt declared. "No offense to you, big guy."

"None taken."

"If there's ever anything I can do for you, Scott, don't hesitate to let me know. I owe your father everything. A lot of us old-timers do."

He smiled again, but the skeptical stare didn't go away. This was beginning to feel like a test, one that I was destined to fail.

"It was nice to have officially met you, commander," I answered as I extended my hand.

Based on Brandt's limp handshake, I knew I'd already failed the test. His eyes brightened as they turned to Kimball. "Nate, always great running into you. If that tie ever starts to feel too tight around your neck, there's some sturdy Kevlar back at HQ with your name on it."

Kimball smiled as if a pleasant memory had washed over him. "I'm sure it fits as snug as ever."

"Damn right it does. But for now, you boys have a job to do, and I'm not going to keep you a second longer. You just make sure–" His ringing cell phone interrupted the thought. "Excuse me while I take this," he said as he stepped away.

Kimball and I exchanged a glance. I detected something in his eyes that I couldn't quite interpret. It could've been anxiety, it could've been irritation. It certainly wasn't good. His cell phone began buzzing before I could ask about it.

He answered on the first ring. "Kimball. You're kidding. Okay, we're on our way." The irritation in his eyes was suddenly gone, replaced with wide-eyed excitement. "Someone called into the snitch-line. We have a beat on Arturo's location. He's holed up in a house in the Park Hill area."

Brandt cut in before I could respond. "I just got the same call. My unit is suiting up now. Smash and grab."

Kimball's smile couldn't have been any wider. "Just like the old days."

"I'll be out in the field myself for this one," Brandt said with a smile as wide as Kimball's. "When an asshole takes a shot at one of my guys, I have to be there when he goes down."

For some reason that wasn't a comforting thought.

"Works for me," Kimball said as he punched my arm. I suddenly had a real-life cowboy on my hands. "Let's go get him."

Brandt led the way back to HQ, the sirens in his car blaring. They were barely loud enough to quiet the sirens going off in my head.

CHAPTER 14

By the time we arrived at the remote briefing location three blocks from the house that Sandoval had barricaded himself in, SWAT was already preparing to move in. The fully armored six-man team stood in a tight circle as one of them ran down the specifics of the operation.

"Remember, this guy took a shot at a detective without a second's hesitation, so stay on your toes when you get in there. Expect the suspect to be armed and ready to move on you. We go in swarming, but we also stay sharp and mind our targets. Understood?"

The other five nodded as they adjusted their helmets, tightened their Kevlar vests, and inspected their assault rifles. These were the certified bad-asses of the DPD, and the rep was well-deserved, as evidenced by the proud-papa grin on Brandt's face as he approached the group.

"Afternoon, Officer Renner. From the look of things, the ship is as tight as ever."

The leader walked up to Brandt. "Hey, commander. We're set to go if you are." He gave Kimball and me a once-over before greeting us with a nod. We'd both traded in our suit jackets for bulletproof vests.

"I think you gentlemen know Detective Kimball, the

traitor, I mean ex-SWAT standout."

A friendly chuckle from the group.

"Thanks for covering us, boys," Kimball said with a slight smile. "In case you didn't know, I'm the detective our friend Sandoval pointed the .357 at, so I'm extra motivated to make this collar."

"We got your back anytime, Kimmy," the leader declared. "Even though you bailed on us—I mean moved on to greater opportunities in homicide."

More laughter. This was starting to feel like a frat party that I wasn't invited to.

Brandt looked at me. "And this here is Kimball's partner, Detective Scott Priest. Even if you don't know Scott, I'm sure you're all familiar with the Priest name, legendary as it is."

I wasn't met with nearly the same enthusiasm as Kimball, but I've never been one for parades in my honor.

Brandt continued. "So, what does your intel say about the location?"

"Even though the curtains over the windows have limited our visibility, there hasn't appeared to be much movement," Officer Renner said. "But we do have confirmation that the suspect is inside, along with an unidentified female Caucasian."

"Entry?"

"Standard double-lock wooden door. No storm screen. Should be easy."

"Do we dare knock first?" Kimball asked sarcastically.

"Apparently that didn't work so well last time," Renner answered with a half-grin.

"Okay men let's get ready to move," Brandt finally told the group. "Remember, in addition to shooting at Detective Kimball, Sandoval is wanted in connection to the murder of Marisol Alvarez. Ms. Alvarez was a hardworking single parent of two teenage girls. She didn't deserve to die the way she did. Let's do what we need to do."

Even though I seriously doubted the sincerity of Brandt's words, I couldn't disagree with the sentiment behind them. I was eager to keep my promise to Marisol's daughters, and the sooner I could get my hands on Arturo, the sooner that promise would be fulfilled.

The look in Kimball's eyes told me just how eager he was too, but I suspected his motives were very different from mine.

"Ready to do this?" he asked as he tightened the shoulder strap of his armored vest.

I took a deep breath before answering. "Nobody in the world I'd rather roll with."

CHAPTER 15

The six bad-asses walked up to the house single-file, their footfalls so light it was as if they weren't touching the ground. The element of surprise was rule number one in the tactical-entry handbook. From the look of it, Arturo Sandoval was in for one nasty surprise.

Officer Renner held point at the front door while the hammer-man fanned off to the left, battering-ram at the ready. Kimball, Brandt, and I brought up the rear, Glocks drawn. We knew it probably wasn't necessary given the heavy artillery between Arturo and us, but SWAT runs present some of the most unstable scenarios that a cop can ever face. That's why they were handled by SWAT.

Renner quickly surveyed his group. Silent nods confirmed their readiness. Renner then looked at the hammer-man and flashed the OK sign.

In an instant, the silence of a calm afternoon was shattered by the sound of splintered wood and the pop of flash grenades. The team entered the house in the same orderly fashion in which they'd approached it, this time with the full intention of making their presence known.

"Denver police!"

"Search warrant!"

"Hands up! Get on the ground!"

The raised voices barking demands seemed to meld into a swarm of angry white noise. Shock and awe at its finest.

Once the last member of the team cleared the doorway, we made our way up the front porch. The scrambling inside continued. Glass was broken. Furniture was toppled. Doors were kicked in. Before I could enter the doorway, Kimball brushed past me with his Glock extended.

A man on a mission.

He sprinted into the sparsely furnished living room and around a corner before I could urge him to slow down.

"Damn it, Nate! They haven't cleared the room yet!"

I looked back at Brandt, wondering exactly why he was here. Based on the unsettled look in his eyes, I guessed he was wondering the same thing. Figureheads had no business in the field, and no matter how many stripes he could sew onto his sleeve, Oliver Brandt was a figurehead.

I turned away from the commander without a word and ambled toward the corner of the house where I last saw Kimball. Heavy footsteps from above shook the ceiling as the chorus of shouting continued.

"*Clear!*"

"*Clear!*"

Just as I rounded the corner to the kitchen where I'd assumed Kimball was, he blew past me on his way up the stairs. "Goddamn it, Nate! They're covering it!"

He didn't reply, choosing instead to let his adrenaline carry him up the stairs two at a time. When he reached the top of the staircase, he muttered something that sounded like, "I know he's here." Then he tore off into a room that Renner and another officer had just entered.

I heard the woman scream as my foot hit the first step. Before I could reach the second, I heard the gunshot. A single 9mm pop. The bad-asses were carrying assault rifles, so the pop couldn't have come from them. Two more pops. If Arturo had taken the shot, the return fire would have been deafening.

Instead, a sudden swell of quiet hung in the air, broken only by the sound of Renner's breathless voice. "Suspect down!"

I promptly stopped. Based on the scenario I was now positive had just played out, I would've done better to turn around, walk back down the stairs and out of the house, but I had to see the sudden disintegration of the Alvarez case with my own eyes.

It was as bad as I thought it would be.

Kimball and Renner stood on either side of Arturo's limp body as the other SWAT officers surrounded the screaming woman.

Renner pulled an officer aside. "Radio it in. Suspect Arturo Sandoval is down. Unidentified female Caucasian in custody."

"Yes sir," the officer replied before patching into his shouldered two-way.

Renner then turned his attention to a motionless Kimball. "You okay?"

"It happened so fast."

"You did the only thing you could do under the circumstances."

Kimball was silent as he re-holstered his weapon.

"You feel confident about that, right?" Renner asked. "That there was nothing else you could've done."

When Kimball turned around to see me staring at him, his faltering face suddenly stiffened. "Absolutely. He was trying to jump out the goddamn window."

"Not to mention the fact that he drew on you,"

Renner added for good measure.

I looked at the area surrounding Arturo's body. I only saw blood. "Where's the piece?"

Officer Renner turned to me like my presence suddenly bothered him. "What?"

"Where is the piece?" I repeated, making sure to annunciate each syllable as clearly as I could.

There was a brief glance between Kimball and Renner before the officer answered. "It went flying out the window after the suspect was hit with the second shot."

"Is that how it happened, Nate?"

Kimball looked at Arturo, then nodded. "Yeah, that's how it happened."

I'd never wanted to believe something more in my entire life. The benefit of the doubt that was a natural byproduct of our friendship should've been enough to ensure that belief. Right now, it wasn't.

"Don't you think we should send someone down there to get it?"

"Not necessary," Brandt declared as he entered the room. A Glock 19 dangled loosely from his gloved finger. "Found it on the side of the house directly under the window."

How convenient. "You sure that's the gun, Nate?"

"What are the odds that we'd find a random gun in the exact spot where his would have landed?"

I ignored the commander's comment. "Nate?"

"Damn sure looks like it."

The definitiveness of his statement was undercut by the doubt in his voice.

Brandt gave the gun to one of the SWAT officers. "Bag it for ballistics. I'm sure we'll get our official confirmation there. Personally speaking, Nathan's word is all the confirmation I need."

"Can't argue with that," Renner said.

After a long silence, Kimball looked at me. "What about you, Scott?"

"What about me, Nate?"

"Are you good with what happened here?"

"Are you?"

"Yes, I am."

"You're good with the fact that we may never close this case because our prime suspect is dead?"

"I'm good with the fact that none of *us* are dead," he snapped back.

"Both of you calm down," Brandt demanded. "This guy pulled out a gun on an officer twice in one day. Innocent people rarely do that. Combine that with the surveillance footage and the sudden availability of DNA, and I'd say your case is still pretty damn solid."

I could only shake my head as I walked out of the room. From the corner of my eye, I saw Kimball following. I didn't turn to acknowledge him, even as he began speaking.

"What the hell is wrong with you, Scott? That son of a bitch tried to take me out twice. I'm sorry if you're upset that he won't have his day in court, but right now I could give two shits about that. As far as I'm concerned, he got exactly what he deserved. It's not like I woke up this morning with the intention of pulling my gun out on anyone, and I'm sure as hell not happy that I had to use it, but he forced my hand. If I hadn't done what I did, you might've been reading my obituary a week from now instead of his. Do you get that?"

"I get that it's entirely too convenient for Commander Brandt to have found that gun so quickly when, as far as I could tell, he hadn't even been up here to see what happened."

When Kimball invaded my personal space for the

second time today, I didn't nudge him away as I'd done the first time.

"What exactly are you trying to say?" His stare didn't waver.

Neither did mine. "I didn't think there was anything ambiguous about it."

"Hey, you guys need to cool it," I heard Renner say. "Clean-up is en route, and they'll be bringing a million questions with them. We need to make sure we're giving them consistent answers. Is consistency going to be a problem for anyone?"

I turned around to see Renner and his army of bad-asses staring at Kimball and me.

"I don't see why it would be," Brandt said as he emerged from behind the group.

Kimball backed out of my face, finally allowing the two of us to breathe. "Neither do I." When he looked at me again, the aggression in his eyes was gone. "You know me better than anyone else, Scott, and you know my word means something. I didn't have a choice."

For a moment, all the doubt and paranoia went away. For a moment, I only saw my friend – the man whose hands I'd most trust my life to be in. And at that moment, I had no choice but to nod my head and say "okay."

As the group made its way outside where patrol units were already gathering, one of the SWAT guys led Arturo's girlfriend to a waiting female officer. The woman was physically and emotionally ravaged, as I suspected she would be. The SWAT officer handed her off with instructions to conduct a thorough body search before the reading of her Miranda's.

As the officer turned her around to execute the pat down, the woman's eyes unexpectedly met mine. They were so swollen from crying I was surprised she could see through them, but it was obvious that she saw me just fine.

"Any needles or other sharp objects?" the officer asked the woman before she stuck her hand in the deep pockets of her soiled overalls.

She didn't reply, choosing instead to keep her focus on me.

"Ma'am? I need to know if you're carrying anything that's gonna stick me."

The woman's response was directed at me, and it was one I wasn't the least bit prepared for.

"Don't believe what they tell you. Not a goddamn word of it."

CHAPTER 16

I managed to slip away from the scene before I could be cornered for an official statement, opting to catch a ride back to HQ with a couple of uniforms. The two young patrol officers, Hicks and D'Agostino, were quiet for the entire drive as if they were hesitant to speak freely in my presence.

My thoughts immediately drifted back to the two officers I'd encountered outside of Marisol's apartment earlier in the day. They were just as inhospitable as these two, and I began to wonder if someone simply took a piss in the morning pot of coffee or if something else was happening; something related to my meeting with Hitchcock and Fitzgerald.

"It's an issue that affects multiple units in the department, from patrol to narcotics to homicide."

Hitchcock's declaration echoed in my head as I watched the officers from the back seat. Were these the kind of guys I was supposed to observe and report on? A couple of no names fresh out of the academy with an unquenchable thirst to clean up the streets and not enough real-world experience to understand the depths of their futility?

Or was I supposed to observe the guys who knew the game? The guys who stood callously over Arturo

Sandoval's dead body as they concocted ways to justify his end?

More to the point, did it even matter who I was supposed to observe? Was it all just process to prove to the brass that something was being done to clean up the problem they were all convinced existed? Did it matter all the more that a cop with the Priest last name was involved in the clean-up?

A million other questions followed these, not one of them containing anything approaching an obvious answer. All I knew for sure as we made the insufferably long drive was that I wanted to get away from these assholes Hicks and D'Agostino as quickly as I could.

*****

I jumped in my own cruiser the moment I got back to HQ, knowing that I was dangerously close to having the department hounds put on my trail. As far as I was concerned, the inquest into Arturo's shooting meant nothing. They could ask all the questions they wanted. I wasn't interested in corroborating Kimball's version of events. He had his army of frat brothers to do that. The only thing that mattered to me was that my suspect was dead, and he took any real hope of closing Marisol's case with him.

I hit the street without a destination in mind. I'd considered paying a visit to Marisol's daughters, but I was certain they would mistake my news as a sign of victory, and the last thing I wanted was empty praise for a job well done. In my mind, the job was far from done.

I'd barely gotten a mile away from HQ when my cell phone began ringing. The hounds were already sniffing. I'd had every intention of ignoring the calls, but as soon as my phone stopped ringing, it started up again. After the fifth cycle of this, I finally took it out of my pocket. The lone name I saw on the message screen was not the one I was expecting.

I redialed Kyle McKenna's number with a surprising lack of hesitation. She answered on the first ring, her heavy breathing making it evident that she'd sprinted to the phone.

"I've been trying like crazy to reach you."

"And I was trying like crazy to avoid you. Guess we know who succeeded."

"What just happened?"

"With what?"

"Arturo."

"Since when are you on a first name basis with my suspect?"

"Since he became a confidential source of mine two months ago."

The only thing that surprised me about Kyle's statement was my lack of surprise in hearing it. "Your confidential source is dead."

"I'm well aware of that."

"Are you also aware that he was the prime suspect in Marisol's murder?"

"Is this how the DPD is dealing with murder suspects now?"

I sighed heavily into the phone. "Somebody really needs to confiscate your police scanner."

"We need to talk, Scott."

"We are talking, Kyle."

"Away from the prying ears of your department cell phone."

At least I wasn't the only one who was paranoid. "I'm three blocks away from the City Perk Café."

"I can meet you there in ten."

CHAPTER 17

I'd just put two large coffees on a far back table when Kyle walked up.

"What the hell?"

"Nice to see you too, dear," I replied with a limp smile, then pointed at her coffee cup. "I hope you don't mind, I took you for a cream, no sugar kind of girl."

"This definitely isn't the time." The scowl on her face affirmed the seriousness of her warning.

I pulled out her chair before sitting in my own. "What do you want me to tell you? The shit got away from us."

"The shit got away from you? Is that the official explanation?"

"I'm sure it will be after the quote ends up in your paper."

Kyle shook her head. "You can deflect with the best of them, I'll give you that."

"Look, you're nowhere near as pissed off about this as I am, okay?"

"Arturo was a friend, so I seriously doubt that."

"You need to choose your friends more carefully."

"And you need to tell me why he's dead."

"Get a grip, Kyle. Even if I wanted to tell you, I

couldn't. You've been around long enough to know that."

"And you've been around me long enough to know that I have an extremely low tolerance for bullshit."

"As do I. So why don't you cut to the chase and tell me why we're sitting here."

Kyle took a long drink of coffee in an apparent effort to steady herself. "It's simple. Arturo knew this was going to happen."

"He knew what was going to happen?"

"That the police were going to kill him."

"And he told you this?" I asked in the calmest voice I could summon.

"I talked to him this morning, not even twenty minutes after I saw you. He told me a lot more about his relationship with the Brandt's, Bethany Brandt specifically."

"Did he also tell you that he planned to shoot a homicide detective who simply wanted to ask him a few questions? Because that's exactly what he tried to do to my partner."

Kyle rolled her eyes. "Of course he didn't tell me that."

"Right. Then maybe you should wait to hear the entire story before you start hurling accusations."

"Well, until you see fit to tell me the entire story, I only have his, and it didn't involve any plans to gun down your partner."

"How is it that you know his story at all?"

For the first time since the conversation began, Kyle hesitated. "He was the source of my information about Marisol and Oliver Brandt."

I'd had a sinking feeling that she was going to say that, though hearing the words aloud felt a whole lot worse. "Go on."

"The two of them had become close from their time working in Brandt's home."

"How close?"

"If you're asking whether or not there was a romantic relationship, I don't have an answer for that. All I know is that they confided in each other quite a bit. In turn, Arturo confided in me."

"About what?"

"His affair with Bethany."

I nearly choked on the sip of coffee I'd just taken. "Affair?"

"That's what this whole thing was about, Scott. The phone conversation that Marisol overheard between Arturo and Oliver Brandt."

"Let me guess, Commander Brandt knew about the affair and threatened to kill Arturo if he didn't end it."

"According to Arturo, the threat wasn't quite that explicit, but it was definitely implied."

"And Marisol was subsequently fired because she overheard this implied threat."

"That's right. When Marisol confronted Arturo about what she'd heard, he admitted everything, including his concern that they would both be targeted by Brandt because of it."

"So Arturo just called you this morning out of the blue to tell you all this?"

"That's usually how it works with confidential sources."

"Why did he choose you in the first place?"

"He'd been following my investigation of Brandt's connection to Detective Graham, and he thought he could offer some useful insights into the man's character."

"I see. So following your line of thinking, both Marisol and Arturo were killed by Brandt in order to keep his wife's affair a secret. Does that about sum it up?"

Kyle sat back in her chair and shook her head, clearly irritated by the level of perceived sarcasm in my voice. "I can see I'm wasting my time here. My fault for not knowing better."

"I'm open to anything, Kyle. You only need to show me proof."

"Where is your proof that Arturo killed Marisol?"

"I imagine most of it will come through a DNA swab. But for now, I have Arturo on surveillance camera entering a hotel suite with Marisol hours before her body was found there."

"And?"

"The .357 Mag casings that Arturo tried to fill Detective Kimball's chest with."

Kyle sighed. "The only thing the former proves is that he and Marisol were possibly sleeping together. The only thing the latter proves is that Arturo believed you were coming to make good on Brandt's threat."

Now I was the one shaking my head. "You're right, Kyle. You're wasting your time here. And now you're wasting mine too."

"You were just at the scene of an officer-involved shooting, which means you should probably be off somewhere giving a statement, but you're here instead. So you obviously thought I had something meaningful to say."

"I did think that until you actually started talking."

"A company man through and through."

"I am until you show me proof that I shouldn't be."

Kyle mumbled something indecipherable as she gathered her coffee and messenger bag and stood up.

I put my hand on her forearm before she could walk away. "Show me proof."

"Have a nice day, detective," she responded as she tried to wiggle away from my grip. I responded by tightening it.

"I'm asking you to show me proof."

The look in my eyes stopped her cold. "You're serious."

I held her stare as I released her arm.

She nodded as she pushed her chair in.

"As far as everything we've talked about here?" I asked as she started to walk away.

"It doesn't leave this table," she assured me.

I had every reason in the world not to trust her.

But right now, there were simply no better options.

CHAPTER 18

I walked back to the car with my sights set on more aimless driving when another phone call came through. This time I knew I couldn't ignore it.

"Hello, Lieutenant."

"What's going on, Scott? Nate is climbing the goddamn walls over here because he can't find you."

"I needed a few minutes to clear my head."

"Clear head or not, you need to come back. Everyone who was at the Sandoval scene is being questioned, and you're the only one unaccounted for."

"How much do you know about what happened?"

"Only what Commander Brandt has told me. But compared to the other statements, it all lines up."

"Great, so why do you need me?"

"I don't make procedure, Scott. Just get here ASAP."

"Fine," I said to a dead phone.

*****

I entered the Major Crimes unit to the sight of Hitchcock and Brandt huddled outside the lieutenant's office. From what I could tell, Brandt was doing all the talking. Both men turned to look at me as I sat down at my desk. Hitchcock acknowledged me with a nod, Brandt with a glare.

When they finished, Hitchcock opened his office door and went inside. The door remained open just long enough for me to spot Kimball sitting in the exact same chair I'd sat in earlier this morning. It was clear that his nerves were no less frayed than mine had been. Hitchcock glanced at me one more time before closing the door.

"Hell of a time for a disappearing act."

I heard Commander Brandt's voice before I realized that he'd walked up to my desk. A cold smile lined his face. "The boys and I were starting to worry that you'd jumped ship."

I resisted the urge to tell him and his boys exactly where they could go. "I have no idea what you're talking about."

Brandt's smile grew. "Of course not, because that isn't the kind of thing you'd do."

"No offense, but how would you know the first thing about what I'd do?"

"Because I knew your father. I knew what kind of cop he was, what kind of man he was. And I knew he raised you and your brother to be the exact same way."

This was the second time in two conversations that he'd brought up my father and brother, and I was suddenly very curious to know why. "How did you know my brother?"

"Through the narc unit, same as your father. He came in around the time Carl was leaving. It's a shame your old man couldn't have stayed on longer. Those two would have made a hell of a duo."

"Were you around when Matt was killed?"

Brandt's frigid smile went away. "It happened just after I took over SWAT. I sure wish I'd been there. Maybe I could've done something to stop it."

I bristled at the comment.

"Sorry, Scott. I know it's a sensitive subject."

"My fault. I never should've brought it up."

"No, I'm actually glad you did."

"Why's that?"

"I always admired the way the two of them handled their business on the street, your father especially. Some of the up and comers around here could learn a lot from him. I certainly did."

I was deathly afraid of where this was going. Unfortunately, that fear wasn't enough to prevent my next question. "What exactly did you learn from him?"

Brandt helped himself to a seat at Kimball's desk. He wheeled the chair close to me before he spoke. "Aside from the obvious stuff about loyalty to the shield, the dangers of bringing the job home, or home to the job, Carl taught me the importance of knowing when to toe the line and when not to. There are situations we encounter out there that require us to make choices. Some choices are easy. Some are difficult. Some threaten to go against the fabric of everything we think we stand for. Whatever that choice is, it's always important to remember that the decision doesn't just affect you. It affects everyone around you. In the case of a police officer, that could mean your partner, your unit, or the entire department.

He paused as he moved his chair closer. "Your father and brother worked the toughest assignment that a cop can face. They saw things every day that the average person couldn't begin to imagine. And they dealt with it. They dealt with it damn well, in fact. They also had to make some tough choices along the way. A lot of times, those choices went against their personal code of ethics. But out here it's not always about your personal code of ethics. It's about getting the job done and making sure the guys in your unit get home safely to their families at night. It's about looking out for this shield and making sure nothing stains it. God knows there are plenty of people out there right now trying to stain it. Kyle McKenna immediately comes to mind. And she's probably going to double her efforts with this whole Sandoval situation. We can't let that happen, Scott. That means we have to stand together on this thing. No matter what you may think, Kimball is your partner. From what he's told me, he's also your friend. Make the right choice for your friend. Prove to people that the apple really doesn't fall far from the tree."

I sat back in my chair and smiled; a vain attempt at suppressing my desire to slam his pasty, bloated face against the edge of the desk. "I don't have anything to prove commander, to you or anyone else. And don't ever compare yourself to my father or brother again."

Brandt's eyes were expressionless as he wheeled the chair back to Kimball's desk and stood up. "So much for the apple," he said before walking away.

More than happy to disappoint you, was my thought as he disappeared into the stairwell.

I'd barely had time to process the encounter when Hitchcock's office door opened. Kimball and the lieutenant walked out together, their expressions equally solemn.

Kimball was the first to make eye contact with me. He held my stare as he said his last words to Hitchcock. I was just out of earshot of the conversation, but I could tell it hadn't gone smoothly. It rarely does with Hitchcock.

The lieutenant gave me a brief look before going back into his office and shutting the door.

My stomach tightened as Kimball approached.

"Where have you been?"

"I had to get a little distance," I answered.

"From what?"

"My own messed up thoughts."

"Did it work?"

"No."

A look of resignation settled over Kimball as he nodded.

"So how did it go in there?" I asked.

"Apparently, the media is already on the story, and they've started camping out downstairs again. The lieutenant seems more worried about the department's press release then he is about helping me get through this."

"The department's in a tough spot, Nate. Has been for a while. This is only going to make things worse. Part of me can't blame him for being worried."

Kimball looked at me with distant eyes. "What about me?"

I felt a momentary surge of guilt as I stared back at him. "Of course I'm worried about you."

"Is that why you took off without saying a word to anyone? Is that why you didn't answer my calls? Is that why you still haven't given your official account of what happened? Because you're so worried about me?"

I brought my hands up to my temples to massage away the pounding in my skull. "Look, I'm sorry that I disappeared on you. There's just a lot going on right now. More than you realize. Brandt is dirty, Nate."

"Not this shit again."

"Just look at everything happening around here right now. Detectives Graham and Sullivan. Marisol. Arturo. What's the common thread there? Commander Brandt. At some point, you have to ask yourself why that is?"

Kimball buried his face in his hands. "I can't have this conversation right now."

"When are we supposed to have it?"

"How about after you go into the lieutenant's office and vouch for the fact that I'm not a goddamn murderer? Something you should've done hours ago."

The pounding in my skull intensified. "I didn't see what happened in there. You know that."

"That shouldn't stop you from saying what needs to be said."

"That's the same thing I heard from Brandt five minutes ago."

The look in Kimball's eyes suddenly hardened. "So that's what this is all about. You don't trust me either."

"Nate hold on a sec-"

He stood up before I could finish.

"You know what I think, Scott? I think it's time to start asking some questions about you. But I'll save that for another time. For now, you just make sure you go in the lieutenant's office and do right by me.

With that, Kimball walked away, taking my last remaining guidepost with him.

CHAPTER 19

The lieutenant's eyes lit up when he opened the door. It was clear he'd been expecting me. "Come in, Scott."

I quickly entered and took a seat in the same chair I'd occupied this morning. It was just as hot now as it was then.

"So where should we start?" Hitchcock asked as he settled behind his desk.

"Not where you think."

"So you won't be giving a statement on the Sandoval shooting?"

"Not if I have to lie about it."

Hitchcock put his notepad and pen down on the desk. "Obviously I don't want you to lie about it."

"But you also want it to go away."

"We all do."

"You have to know that it's not going away."

Hitchcock looked irritated as he sat back in his chair and crossed his arms. "Get to it."

"Your offer from this morning."

"What about it?"

I didn't hesitate. "I'm in."

The lieutenant uncrossed his arms and leaned forward. His mouth creased with the thinnest of smiles. "Are you sure? Circumstances being what they are now?"

"I'm sure *because* of the circumstances being what they are now."

"If you need more time, you still have until the morning to decide."

"Not necessary."

Hitchcock paused as if he were giving me one last opportunity to change my mind. My continued silence prompted him to go forward. "I'll get Robert Fitzgerald on the phone, and the three of us will meet here tomorrow as scheduled. In the meantime, what do you plan to do about Kimball?"

I shrugged. "Maybe that'll come up in the meeting tomorrow."

"What exactly do you mean by that?"

I wasn't sure. I only knew that I instantly regretted saying it. "I'm not in a position to give a statement on the Sandoval shooting right now. I'm still trying to deal with the fact that my lone suspect is dead."

Hitchcock nodded. "I guess your case is in a bit of a tailspin."

"That's an understatement."

Hitchcock stood up from his desk, walked over to his file cabinet, and pulled out a thin manila folder. "Probably not the best time to take on something like this, but I suppose there's never really a good time." He set the folder on the desk.

I knew he'd put it there for me, but I didn't want to touch it. "What's that?"

"A pre-briefing ahead of tomorrow's meeting. We're taking this thing in stages, scrutinizing every cog in the wheel independently. That file represents the first cog."

My breath caught as images of Brandt and Kimball darted around in my head. I blocked out Kimball's face as quickly as it came, but Brandt lingered, as did my fear of Hitchcock's reaction to my intention of pursuing the commander as an accessory to Marisol Alvarez's murder.

The thought went away the second I opened the folder.

"What the hell is this?"

"Exactly what it looks like," Hitchcock said bluntly.

I had to look twice more at the name on the front of the file. It still didn't register as being real. "What does Chloe Sullivan have to do with this?"

"Internal Affairs had been on Walter Graham's ass for years. They were this close to plugging him on evidence tampering and several other charges when the case magically went away. Two weeks after that, Graham and Sullivan were shot. Given the circumstances of the shooting, the timing of it, and Detective Sullivan's unwillingness to talk about it beyond her official statement, she's found herself smack dab in the middle of the Attorney General's radar screen. Not the best place to be right now."

I suddenly felt sick to my stomach. "Is everybody forgetting that she was almost killed?"

"No one is forgetting that, Scott. They simply want to know *why* she was almost killed."

"So because she was Graham's partner and she happened to find herself in the wrong place at the wrong time, she's suddenly a criminal? From what I know about the Elliott Richmond case, she was basically the one who cracked the damn thing."

"It doesn't seem like you're entering this with a very open mind," Hitchcock contended.

I closed the folder without reading anything more. "I just thought you'd be going in a different direction with this."

"And what direction would that be?"

I felt my face drop as I stood up. "I guess it's not really important."

I made it halfway out the door before Hitchcock responded. "Full briefing tomorrow morning at 9:30. Maybe you'll have a better understanding of things after that."

My doubt could not have been more overwhelming.

As I left his office, I thought about my dad's words of warning. "*Stay out of the tall weeds. Believe me, you won't like what's in there.*"

I wasn't sure at what point I'd stepped into those weeds, but there was no denying that I was chest deep now. And just like he predicted, I didn't like what I saw one bit.

CHAPTER 20

I normally enter my apartment building to all manner of smells, from the stairwell that's regularly used as a urinal to the peasant stew that is the staple of the Eastern European immigrants who live down the hall. But I've never opened my door to the smell of fresh pasta sauce and garlic bread. The aroma was as comforting after a long, miserable day as any I could've imagined, even though its presence made me put a hand to my shoulder holster. I live alone and shouldn't have smelled anything in my apartment other than the dirty laundry I was two weeks behind on.

"Scott? Is that you?"

I heard her voice before I saw her face. My hand dropped from the butt of my gun, just as my heart dropped from my chest. "It's me."

When I entered the kitchen, she was standing over the stove with her back to me, steam rising over her shoulder. She was wearing the yoga pants and form-fitting tee shirt that had been the cornerstone of her day-off wardrobe, and even though I couldn't see her face, she seemed very happy to be here. Had this been any other day, I would've been just as happy. But because it was today, all I wanted was to run away from her and her surprise dinner as quickly as I could.

"I took the liberty of using the key you gave me once upon a time. I hope that's okay," she said as she dipped a spoon in the pot of red sauce.

"Of course."

She was smiling as she turned and approached me with the spoon. "Taste this. I figure it's the first bit of real food you've had in at least a week."

It had probably been longer. "Delicious," I said after she slid the spoon out of my mouth. "Four cheese and garlic?"

Detective Chloe Sullivan nodded. "Your favorite if I remember correctly."

I took off my jacket and shoulder holster and went into the kitchen. "Anything I can do to help?"

"Nope. Almost finished. It's great that you're here. I wasn't sure when you'd be back, so I just planned on leaving a note."

I finally allowed room for the smile that should've naturally come over my face. "I appreciate the gesture. Thank you."

"You're welcome."

When she looked at me something in my chest fluttered, the same as it had every time she looked at me. Without saying a word, she pulled me into her space. Despite the heaviness that was about to enter our conversation, the world felt one hundred percent perfect as my hand moved up the delicate contours of her back to her neck and finally through her mane of curly brown hair. As she brought her soft lips to mine, I could taste fresh parmesan cheese and a hint of red wine. For a moment, I forgot about everything. Then she pulled back to allow me a long glance into her bright hazel eyes, and the awfulness came flooding back.

"Do you want to get cleaned up while I get a couple of plates? I've had a three-day break from HQ, and I'm sure there's a ton of craziness you need to catch me up on."

"That's putting it mildly," I answered with a painfully uncomfortable smile.

Chloe and I had only been dating for three months, but she could already read me better than anyone else on the planet, Nate included. "Oh boy. Do we need something stiffer than Pinot with dinner?"

"Probably."

"Is it concerning the Alvarez case? Last I heard she was formally identified on the news this morning. I've been holed up in your kitchen ever since so I may be a little behind."

"It started out being about the case. Then it became something else. Something more personal."

The brightness in her eyes slowly dimmed. My heart ached with the knowledge that I was about to darken them entirely. "What?"

"It became about you."

Nerves caused her slim frame to shiver as she walked to the cabinet and took out two plates. "Let me guess, our secret relationship suddenly became not-so-secret. Was it Nathan who finally figured it out?"

"It's not anything like that."

She put the plates on the counter and turned to me, her tolerance for the suspense clearly running out. "Then what is it about?"

"It's about me, you, and Walter Graham."

Without saying a word, Chloe abandoned the plates and took a seat at the dining room table. She stared straight ahead, like someone in shock attempting to detach themselves from the terrible news they were about to receive. I'd seen the look on the faces of victims and their families a million times before. The news wouldn't be any easier to deliver this time.

"What about Walter?" she asked in a faraway voice.

I sighed as I walked to the cabinet where I kept a stash of Jameson and my set of Glencairn whiskey glasses. "We absolutely need something stiffer than the Pinot. This is going to be a very long conversation."

*****

Two hours and half a bottle of Jameson later, Chloe and I were still sitting at the table. The food that she'd gone through so much trouble to prepare hadn't been touched. Neither of us felt much like eating.

"I guess this is the thanks I get for taking a bullet in the line of duty," she said in a flat tone. Her face was punctuated with the disbelief that you'd expect out of an innocent person who learns they're being investigated for possible criminal activity.

"This doesn't have anything to do with you," I tried to assure her. "They're grasping at anything they possibly can since Walter isn't here to answer for himself. You were his partner for less than six months, and anyone with two eyes knew that he wasn't thrilled to be paired with you. No offense."

"None taken."

"You didn't have the first clue of what he was up to until the end, and once you found out, you were fully prepared to make him answer for it. Hitchcock knows that."

"Then why isn't he calling off the AG?"

Unfortunately, I didn't have a good answer for that. "I'll make sure you don't get touched by any of this."

"How, Scott? You're the one who's supposed to be spying on me."

"Because now I know where to point the lens."

Chloe took in a nervous breath and slowly let it out. It did little to stop her shaking. "This is Commander Brandt we're talking about. You might as well tell me you're going after Chief Connolly next."

"If that's what it takes," I answered boldly.

"You're walking into dangerous territory here."

"I've been in dangerous territory for a long time, Chloe. The only thing that's changed is that I finally know how to navigate my way out of it. If Hitchcock and Fitzgerald want me to do their dirty work for them, fine. But I'm going to blow the lid off the whole goddamned thing."

"Brandt is an obvious target, but you could end up taking a whole lot of other people down with him – people you care about. Are you prepared to do that?"

Kimball immediately came to mind, but I quickly shook the thought away.

"They can come after me as much as they want," she continued. "I didn't do anything wrong, so nothing they accuse me of will ultimately stick. But a lot of other people have gotten their hands dirty, even if it's with a minor kickback here or a missing piece of evidence there. You can definitely blow the lid off, but if you keep stirring the pot, something's going to bubble up to the surface that you may not want to see. What are you going to do then?"

"Are you saying I shouldn't go through with this?"

"I'm not saying that at all. You have to follow your conscience. But you also need to be careful. They gave you my name, a detective in your own unit, as someone they're possibly investigating, without a shred of proof that there's anything worth investigating. But there wasn't a single mention of Brandt and his connection to the man who killed Walter and tried to kill Camille Grisham and me. They know more about that then they're letting on, but they'd never tell you that. They want you focused on low-hanging fruit because they want to divert the attention away from where it belongs."

"Exactly, so now you know why I want to pursue Brandt myself."

"But they don't want that. If you do find something substantial on Brandt and you take it to Hitchcock or any of the other higher-ups, do you really think they'll do anything with it other than turn it back on you somehow? I admire what you're doing here, and nobody wants to see Brandt get what's coming to him more than I do. But I care about you, and I don't want to see you get yourself into something that you can't get out of."

Chloe's argument was starting to make too much sense, and it scared me, but I also didn't see a way to stop the wheels I'd already set in motion. "I have a contact at the Mile-High Dispatch. If Hitchcock and the

AG don't want to hear what I have to say, I'll go over their heads and say it to the public directly."

Chloe let out a heavy sigh. "You're really prepared to deal with that garbage newspaper? After the bullshit they've written about us?"

"Some of it isn't bullshit."

"This can only end badly," Chloe said in a resigned tone, traces of emotion spilling onto her face.

I got up from the table and made my way over to her. I knelt down and wrapped my arms around her with the intention of not letting go for a long time. "My only concern right now is protecting you. Hitchcock bringing me into this is the best possible thing that could've happened. Without that, we may not have known about their pursuit of you until it was too late. At least this way we can stay ahead of it."

"I already told you, it's not me I'm worried about."

When I looked into her eyes, I realized for the first time just how deep her worry was. I also realized that this was one of those crossroads moments that a person only encounters once or twice in their life. There were two voices in my head vying for attention; both equally strong in their position. One voice preached self-preservation, the other encouraged self-sacrifice. I listened to the well laid-out arguments of both, but the decision had long-since been made. I simply needed the other side – the side that favored self-preservation – to know that it had been heard.

There was only one road to walk now. God only knew where it would lead, but I knew with every ounce of conviction in me that I had to find out.

CHAPTER 21

I knew there wouldn't be much sleep to be had that night, even with Chloe's calming presence next to me. So when the late-night call came in that Arturo's girlfriend was prepared to give a statement on his involvement in Marisol's murder, I was more than ready.

By the time I arrived at HQ, Kimball, Krieger, and Parsons were already gathered inside the observation room. Through the closed-circuit monitor, I could see a nervous Clarissa Dunlap and a man I'd assumed was her legal counsel.

The three detectives eyed me with wary relief as I took a seat next to them.

"Looks like we bagged this one, Scott," Kimball said with a broad smile. "She's ready to give up Arturo in exchange for not being hit with an aiding and abetting charge. We can still slap her with possession of narcotics, but that'll be a walk in the park compared to the time she was looking at."

"And her lawyer has already signed off on this?" I asked with a skepticism that I couldn't explain.

"Lock, stock, and barrel," Krieger said. "All we have to do now is go in there and get the particulars on the record."

"And has anyone told Hitchcock? I figured he'd want to be here to see this closed out, given what happened today."

Kimball met my question with one of his own. "Why would we need to tell him? This is our case."

The three of them looked at me as if they were expecting an immediate answer. Resisting the overwhelming urge to give them one, I quickly changed the subject.

"Who's going in?"

Krieger and Parsons looked at Kimball then back at me.

"It obviously can't be Nate," Krieger answered. "That only leaves you, Baywatch."

I'd had a feeling he was going to say that. "But I was there when Arturo got shot just like Nate was. She walked right past me when she was led out in cuffs." I instantly recalled her words as she made eye contact with me. *"Don't believe what they tell you. Not a goddamn word of it."* I'd hoped to have the chance to talk to Clarissa, but for very different reasons than this. If she had legit evidence pointing to Arturo, I couldn't risk her shutting down. "If you want her to walk out of here without telling us a damn thing, send in the partner of the man who shot her boyfriend."

"She's already stated that she saw nothing and has no plans to offer a witness statement regarding the shooting, except to confirm that Arturo was previously in possession of the Glock found on scene," Parsons reported.

"Still, Scott is absolutely right," Kimball replied quickly. "We need it to be you two. Too many conflicts of interest with Scott and me." He looked in my direction, but my eyes were focused the monitor. A thousand thoughts went through my head as I stared at Clarissa, but one thought demanded attention above all the others, and the more I attempted to suppress it, the louder it got. Who convinced her to keep quiet about what she saw? And more importantly, *how* did they convince her? I couldn't bring myself to think that Nate had any hand in it.

When Krieger and Parsons entered the interview room, Clarissa sat upright in her chair and folded legs the size of twigs into her chest; a defensive posture that communicated her readiness to fend off the impending onslaught that was coming her way.

After taking his seat next to her, Parsons was the first to speak. "My name is Detective Jim Parsons with DPD Homicide. This is Detective Alan Krieger. We'd like to start out by thanking you for agreeing to cooperate with us. Does counsel have any questions before we get started?"

"No questions," the haggard public defender replied. He rubbed at his bloodshot eyes as if all he wanted to do was take off his ill-fitting suit and go to bed. "As long as we're still in agreement about the details of the plea recommendation, we can proceed with Ms. Dunlap's statement."

"We've spoken to the DA via telephone, and she's agreed to the terms of the deal," Krieger confirmed. "Charges of aiding and abetting and harboring a fugitive will be dropped in exchange for your statement, and subsequent testimony should it ever go to court. We'll make it official in the morning."

"In that case, my client is ready to talk."

"Thank you, counselor," Parsons said before turning to Clarissa. "Can I offer you anything, Ms. Dunlap? Coffee? Tea? Soda?"

She blew a wisp of dirty blond hair from her pock-marked ravaged face. "What I really need is a smoke. Can I smoke in here?"

"No, Ms. Dunlap, you can't smoke in here," Krieger answered stiffly. "What you can do is tell us about your boyfriend Arturo Sandoval and Marisol Alvarez."

Clarissa rested her chin on her bony knees. She was the picture of calm. Too calm for my liking. "First off, that asshole wasn't my boyfriend."

"What was he?" Parsons asked.

"Someone I had sex with and did drugs with, and he was really good at both."

All three men inside the room shifted uncomfortably in their chairs.

"What do you know about his relationship with Marisol?" Parsons asked.

"They were fucking too," she said matter-of-factly. "But they also worked together, first at some rich lady's house, then at the Four Seasons Hotel."

"Did he do drugs with Marisol too?" Krieger asked.

Clarissa shook her head. "He says he tried to get her to smoke some pot once, but she was clean. According to him, she didn't even drink. I never knew he was into the square types." Her face suddenly contorted. "Then again, he killed her, so I guess he wasn't that into her."

Kimball and I exchanged a glance. He smiled and looked like he wanted to say something self-congratulatory. I turned my attention back to the monitor before he could.

When I looked in her face, I saw no sadness, no remorse, and no genuine emotion. I only saw a nervous young girl eager to deliver her lines precisely as she'd practiced them. None of it felt real.

"Tell us how you know that Arturo killed Marisol."

Clarissa took a bite out of one of her nails before answering. "Because he came knocking on my door early this morning all bug-eyed and paranoid. I thought he'd been up late binging on something, but after he started talking to me, I knew he was totally sober."

"What was he saying?" Parsons asked.

Kimball grabbed my shoulder. "Here it comes," he beamed. It was as if he knew exactly how she was going to answer. Maybe he did.

"First, he told me that he had some stuff that he needed to stash away, and he wanted to use my place. I told him that if it was a lot of drugs, he couldn't. I wasn't trying to get busted for intent to distribute. He promised me it wasn't drugs, so I said okay."

"Then what?"

"When he brought the bag in, he started rummaging through it, like he was looking for something. That's when I saw the blood."

Parsons' eyes widened. "The blood?"

"Yeah, on the jacket he stuffed in there. It was only for a second, but I saw it plain as day. That's when I asked him about it."

"Go on," Krieger directed.

"He wouldn't tell me anything at first, but I told him that he could trust me, no matter what. I'd never judge him. God knows I'm the last person to judge someone. So, he told me everything."

"About Marisol?"

Clarissa nodded. "He said they met up at the hotel, even though he wasn't scheduled for work. He said that she was the one who told him to meet her there inside one of the fancy suites, which didn't make a lot of sense to me, but whatever. He thought she wanted to hook up, but once they got there, she flipped the script, started freaking out on him about sleeping with some rich lady they used to work for."

Kimball and I looked at each other again, this time I didn't turn away. "Looks like the smoke just became a fire."

Kimball didn't respond.

"That's when Arturo said she started attacking him," Clarissa continued. "According to him, she was going crazy, slapping him, kicking him, biting him. He said he took it for a while, but eventually, he had to fight back."

Parsons leaned into the table. His expression darkened. "So he stabbed her seventeen times?"

Clarissa leaned away from him. "I guess so."

"Where did he get the knife?" Krieger asked.

"He always carried a pocketknife with him for protection. I believe that's what he used."

"He told you that?"

"I saw it in the bag with his bloody jacket."

"Where's the bag?" Parsons asked.

Clarissa looked at her lawyer, suddenly unsure if she should answer. When he nodded his approval, she took a deep breath and continued. "My cousin works for a landfill out by the airport and Arturo wanted me to take it there to get rid of it. I told him I would, we smoked a little something together, and he left. But I never made it to the landfill."

"Where did you put it?" Krieger asked.

She once again hesitated before answering. "In the dumpster of an apartment building two blocks from my place. I was nervous that if he ever found out I'd put it there, he'd kill me too." Her pale blue eyes narrowed. "I guess you guys took care of that problem for me."

I looked at Kimball. Cold eyes stared into the monitor as he covered his mouth to stifle the outburst that was surely begging to be unleashed.

"We need you to tell us where that dumpster is," I heard Parsons say.

"I might be better off showing you. I hid the bag really good."

Parsons looked at Krieger with a flash of excitement. "We can go right now."

Krieger nodded. "I'll call a patrol out to secure the site ahead of our arrival."

Kimball slapped me on the back, barely able to contain his enthusiasm. "I told you we bagged it." Without saying anything else, he stood up, grabbed his jacket, and walked out of the room.

I continued watching Clarissa. Her hands shook; something I hadn't noticed before. Perhaps the gravity of what she'd done had finally hit her. But it was entirely too late for second thoughts now. "I need you guys to do something for me first," she said in a voice that cracked with exhaustion. "I need that cigarette."

Krieger smiled. "You find us that knife, and I'll give you the whole damn carton."

CHAPTER 22

The dim glow of a distant pale moon created an appropriately dour atmosphere as we approached the scene. Patrol units had already blocked off the wide alley behind the apartment building by the time we arrived, while floodlighting had been set up around the dumpster.

Kimball and I watched from the car while Parsons and Krieger led Clarissa and her lawyer past the crime scene tape.

A white van pulled up behind us. Kimball looked in the rear-view mirror and said, "Looks like forensics is already here. Once the knife is found, they should be able to get a quick hit on Arturo's DNA, and that'll put the final stamp on it."

"You seem pretty confident," I said as two CSIs climbed out of the van and approached the dumpster. "There isn't any part of you that's worried she's playing us?"

"Why should she play us? It's her ass on the line. If this doesn't pan out, she's going away for a long time."

"Not very many hours ago, it was our asses on the line. What changed to make her suddenly not see Arturo getting shot?"

If Kimball's looks could kill, I'd be slumped over in the passenger's seat of his car. "She didn't see anything. She told us that, she told her lawyer that. I'm curious what leads you to believe otherwise?"

I watched Clarissa stick her head inside the dumpster as I pondered Kimball's question. She began rummaging through the contents inside. "She said something to me as she was being led out of the house."

"What?"

I turned to him, my stare matching his in its intensity. "Not to believe a word I heard about why Arturo was shot."

Kimball turned away from me and laughed. "Seriously, Scott? How was that enough to make you even *consider* questioning what happened out there? She's a meth-head who was probably jacked out of her mind. Why would you believe a damn thing she said?"

"We're choosing to believe her now. What's the difference?"

On cue, she emerged from her dumpster dive holding a dark-colored backpack, which she promptly handed to Parsons.

"This is a helluva lot different," Kimball snapped.

Parsons opened the bag, slowly pulled out its contents, and placed them on a small tarp that one of the CSIs had laid on the ground. Even from our distant vantage point, it was easy to see the blood-soaked windbreaker, blue jeans, and running shoes. When he took out the Colorado Rockies baseball hat that I'd seen Arturo wearing on the surveillance footage, I blew out an audible sigh. "And for the record, I'm not questioning you."

"Sure sounds that way from where I'm sitting."

When I looked at Kimball again, something in his eyes had changed. The hard edge was gone. It had been replaced with the confused gaze of someone desperate for clarity. At that moment, I once again only saw the friend whom I'd come to trust more than anyone else in the world.

"A lot is going on with me personally right now, and it's skewed my perspective a little more than it should have. I'm sorry for how it's come across."

A flood of relief washed over his face. "You don't have to apologize. We're all under a shitload of stress right now. I had no idea you were taking on more. Why didn't you tell me?"

"I wanted to, but with everything that's gone on today, there wasn't much time."

"Now is as good a time as any, my friend. What's going on?"

Before I could begin to frame my complicated answer, I saw the medium-sized pocket knife in Parsons' hand. He held it high by the tip of the handle and turned it to us. Kimball acknowledged his thumbs-up with a single flash of his headlights. He turned to me with a smile as wide as I'd ever seen it. "Hell yes, Scott. We got him."

I couldn't deny the feeling of satisfaction that came over me as I watched Parsons place that knife on the tarp, though I tempered it the best I could. "I'm sure he tried to wipe it down."

"Forensics should still be able to extract enough to type for Marisol's blood. They don't need much."

I nodded then turned my focus back to Kimball's question; a question I now realized I should've answered hours ago. "My meeting with Hitchcock this morning."

"What about it?"

"We weren't talking about my father."

Kimball looked at me like he already knew that. "Must've been pretty damn serious if you had to lie to me about it."

"Again, I'm sorry about that. At the time I didn't feel like I had a choice."

"And now?"

"Now I don't have a choice but to tell you everything."

And that was exactly what I did. From the tense exchanges with Robert Fitzgerald to the request made by Hitchcock to the revelation that Chloe was a focal point of their current investigation, I ran down the meeting blow for blow. After I finished, I took a breath to allow the entire chain of events to sink in fully. It was only then that I'd come to appreciate just how absurd the whole ordeal really was.

Kimball apparently shared my assessment. "That's the biggest crock of shit I've heard in my entire life."

"Which part?" I asked in a feeble attempt at humor that was clearly misplaced.

"How about the part where Hitchcock asked you to rat out the entire unit? Or the part where he showed you the file on Chloe? She took a bullet for this damn department. Does that not count for anything?"

"Obviously it doesn't," I muttered.

"Is he aware that you two are involved?"

"No. If he did, it would've come up in the meeting."

"Jesus, of all the people he could have a vendetta against."

"I'm not worried about Chloe," I told him. "They've got nothing on her because she's done nothing. Her biggest sin was accepting the offer to partner with Graham in the first place. And I also have no intention of ratting out anyone in our unit. That's not what this is about for me."

Kimball's eyes grew wide. "Tell me you're not considering going through with this."

"I am," I answered firmly.

"What in God's name for?"

"Commander Brandt."

Kimball blew out a loud breath as he choked the steering wheel. "I shouldn't have asked."

"I'm sorry if you don't like it, Nate. But Brandt has a connection to Joseph Solomon and Elliott Richmond. I can't prove that yet, but I know he does, which means he also has a connection to Graham's murder. I talked to Chloe about it, and she feels the same way. And if there's anyone whose opinion should be listened to on the

150

subject, it's hers." I didn't dare mention my suspicion of his involvement in Marisol's murder. I'd save that revelation for another time.

Kimball took a moment to consider his response. "Okay. Let's just say for the sake of argument that you did find something on Brandt and you thought it was worth pursuing. Do you plan to take him down all by yourself? Because if Hitchcock and the Attorney General's office were really interested in going after him, they would've done it already. Commander Brandt has been doing questionable shit for years, but that doesn't change the fact that he's well-liked and incredibly well-connected. I can't lie, Scott, I'm one of those people who likes him. He's been nothing but good to me my entire career."

"So have I."

Kimball rolled his eyes. "That was a low-blow."

"I'm just asking you to trust me as much as I trust you."

"That trust has always cut both ways, you know that."

"Then make sure this situation is no exception."

"I trust you unconditionally, Scott. Always have, always will."

"Good, because I really need that right now."

Silence momentarily settled over us as we watched Krieger lead Clarissa and her lawyer back to the car. Clarissa looked as if her rail-thin legs would give out at any moment. It had been an incredibly long day for her. It had been an incredibly long day for us too.

"I need to ask you one thing though," Kimball said, abruptly breaking the silence.

"I'm listening."

"What if you walk into Hitchcock's office tomorrow and he gives you a file on me? What would you do with it?"

"The same thing I plan to do with Chloe's," I said, fully aware that I wouldn't have been able to answer that question with any confidence a few short hours ago.

"No matter what you saw inside that file?" Kimball reiterated.

This may have been nothing more than a test, but he was making me nervous nonetheless. "Is there something I should know about?"

He was quiet for a long time before answering. "There's something in everyone's file, Scott. It's all a matter of when they decide to turn the microscope on you and how closely they want to look."

"I have no desire to look."

I couldn't tell whether his weak smile was a sign of relief or skepticism.

"I really need you to trust me on that," I continued. "I can't say for certain where this is all going. It might be a bunch of smoke that leads to nothing, and in a week, it'll be like we never even had this conversation. But I want you to know that I've always got your back. No matter what. Now I need to know that you've got mine. I need to know that you'll support me no matter where this ends up. I need to know that I can trust that this conversation never leaves this car. I need to know that you and I can return to business as usual, the same partners that we always were. The same friends that we always were."

We watched as Krieger's car took off down the alley on its way back to HQ. We'd most likely stick around to get an up-close look at the evidence that had now been turned over to forensics. But not before Kimball answered my question.

"Are we the same as we ever were, Nate?"

After another moment of contemplation, Kimball took his hand off the steering wheel, curled it up in a tight fist, and held it out in front of me. "Same as we ever were, my man."

I smiled as I bumped his fist with my own. And as we got out of the car to inspect for ourselves the evidence that represented the end of the Marisol Alvarez case, I was relieved to know that things would stay the same between us. Even if it was only for tonight.

CHAPTER 23

It was nearly two-thirty in the morning by the time I got home. I was relieved to see Chloe still fast asleep in my bed, and I climbed in next to her without so much as taking off my shoes. When I wrapped my arms around her waist, she stirred slightly and settled comfortably into my embrace. Her warmth calmed the racing in my mind almost instantly, and I was asleep before I realized I was even tired.

The warmth of Chloe's presence had been replaced with the warmth of the mid-morning sun by the time I returned to awareness. I was still in my polo shirt and jeans, but my shoes were off. Probably Chloe's doing. When I turned over to check the alarm clock, I saw the handwritten note.

Chloe had apologized for leaving, explaining that she needed to report to the scene of a suicide she was investigating and couldn't stick around. She told me she'd made an egg and avocado scramble, which I could now smell, and wished me well with Hitchcock.

Shit. I forgot all about him.

My eyes drifted to the alarm clock and the time of 10:17 A.M. and I knew exactly what would happen next. I'd walk into the living room, pick up my cell phone, and see the bombardment of missed calls and voicemails. With a sudden shot of adrenaline coursing through my body, I got out of bed and retrieved the phone.

Sure enough, I was right.

The last call (and sixth overall) came in ten minutes ago. I was positive the seventh would follow shortly. But at this point, I was too tired to care.

My adrenaline shot ebbing, I stumbled into the kitchen to pour a cup of the dark roast that Chloe had brewed, then I warmed up a plate of eggs. I took my sweet time eating.

It was nearly noon when I finally walked into HQ. Hitchcock hadn't called me again, and I didn't bother to check any of the three voicemails he left, so I had no idea how I'd be received when I knocked on his door. I walked past my desk on the way to Hitchcock's on the off-chance that Kimball was there. I was relieved to see his empty chair.

There were no nerves when I knocked on the lieutenant's door. I was nearly three hours late to a meeting that I wanted no part of anyway. If that was a punishable offense, I was fully prepared to turn in my gun and badge and not look back.

Instead of reading me the riot act that I probably deserved, Hitchcock smiled as he opened the door.

"So you are alive," he quipped as he stepped aside to allow me in. "I was worried we'd find you in a ditch somewhere."

I thought the joke was in poor taste given the situation but thought it best not to protest. "They haven't found a way to make me disappear yet," I said as I sat.

There was no smarmy bureaucrat behind Hitchcock's desk this time. "I take it Fitzgerald got tired of waiting?"

"Yeah. Didn't you get my voicemails?"

"I figured you'd be yelling, so I didn't bother to listen. I prefer to be scolded in person."

"No scolding, Scott. Not today."

"So you're not pissed that I didn't show up on time?"

"It bugged Fitzgerald a lot more than me. I figured you had a good reason."

"We closed out the Alvarez case last night, and the paperwork kept me up for a while."

"Congratulations."

I nodded, knowing I wasn't deserving of any kudos.

"What now?" he asked.

"The DA should sign off on Clarissa Dunlap's plea deal today if she hasn't already. After that, I'll pay a visit to Marisol's daughters to deliver the news."

"I'm sure they'll be relieved."

I doubted it. I wasn't delivering Brandt's head on a platter like they would have wanted.

"I'm sure you're relieved too," I said. "Arturo's shooting became fully justified before the story could gain much traction. One less stain on the department."

Hitchcock smiled again, only this time I suspected he was masking something much darker. "Speaking of which, what are we doing about this?" He picked up the file on Chloe that he showed me yesterday. "Fitzgerald is dying to know."

"Nothing," I answered firmly.

"Come again?"

"Chloe doesn't have anything to do with the situation you're investigating, and neither do most of the detectives in this unit. You know it, and I know it. So until you and Fitzgerald acknowledge that, I can't help in the way you need me to."

Hitchcock let out a heavy sigh. "So you're prepared to do nothing?"

"I didn't say that."

"What exactly are you saying?"

"You obviously have a lot of faith in me. If you didn't, I wouldn't be sitting here."

"No question."

"Then show enough faith to let me help you the way *I* need to."

"And what does that look like?"

I looked at Chloe's file. "It starts by putting that back in your locked cabinet where it belongs."

"Not until you give me a good reason.

"I plan to. I just need a little time."

Hitchcock gave the file a wary once-over before turning back to me. "Am I going to like what you plan on telling me next?"

"You're hard to please in general, lieutenant, so I doubt it."

That was enough to inspire a tension-cutting smile. "What about Fitzgerald?"

"He's a slimy bastard."

"That goes without saying. What should I tell him about your role in this little project of ours?"

"As far as I'm concerned, he's on a need-to-know basis, at least for now."

"That won't hold water for long."

"Hopefully I won't need much time."

Hitchcock shifted in his chair. "I don't like being left in the dark, but if you're asking for some space with this, you got it. Just know that you're on an extraordinarily short leash, and I expect to be looped into whatever this is very soon."

"Absolutely," I said, meaning it.

"Short leash," Hitchcock reiterated. "If you don't give me just cause to look elsewhere very soon, I'm pursuing the original course, and the benefit of the doubt you've enjoyed up until now will be long gone. Understood?"

I recognized a threat when I heard one, but I was in no position to fight it. "Loud and clear, boss."

"And nothing less than full confidentiality will be acceptable. It's not just your ass on the line here."

That ship had long since sailed, but there was no reason he needed to know that. "Of course."

"Good." After a much-needed silence, he asked, "How are things with you and Nate?"

"Just fine," I said, hoping the nervous twitch I couldn't suppress wasn't enough to expose the lie.

"You two certainly made quick work of the Alvarez case."

"Alan and Jim helped out a lot."

"It takes a team to get most cases solved, and we've got a helluva good team in Major Crimes. I'd like to keep it that way."

"So do I."

When Hitchcock didn't immediately respond, I got the feeling he was gauging my body language for signs of dissonance. Fortunately, I knew exactly what he'd be looking for and fought hard to keep it in check.

"Does that mean the two of you are ready to take on another case? The more you can give off the illusion of business as usual, the easier this thing is going to be for you."

The *illusion* of business as usual. He couldn't have possibly said it any better because we both knew that once I stepped foot outside this office, business would never be the same. "We're ready."

"All things being equal, I'd rather have you solving homicides than going on some covert crusade to help flush out corruption within our department. But I suppose the present climate requires you to do both."

I breathed in deep to test the conviction of what I was about to say. The air went cleanly into my lungs with no effort or constriction. I knew then that I was absolutely ready.

"I wouldn't have it any other way."

CHAPTER 24

A second trip to see my father hadn't been part of the plan before yesterday, but a whole hell of a lot had changed since yesterday.

There were two reasons why I wanted to see him. First, I wanted to give him the news about the Alvarez case. Second, and more importantly, I wanted to let him know just how tall the weeds had grown. Though he always kept the specifics of his work on the force close to the vest (this was especially true of his stint in narcotics) I got the feeling that he'd stumbled his way into more than a few rough patches during his day and could offer me some proper navigation tips. The one thing I feared hearing from him was the dreaded *I told you so*, but if I was going to lean on him to get me through something this heavy, the least I could do was allow him that one indulgence. Frankly, I was prepared to endure a thousand *told you so's* if that's what was required as compensation for his services.

What I wasn't prepared for was the sound of distress in my mother's voice when I told her that I'd just entered the facility and was on my way up to see them.

"I don't think you should, Scott," was her immediate response.

"Why not? Dad told me to come by when I had news about the case we were talking about yesterday. I think he'd like to hear about it."

"Honey, dad won't remember that you were even here yesterday. He may not remember who you are at all."

My first and only reaction was denial. In the two years since his diagnosis and the three months since his descent into full-blown dementia, I'd never seen him at his worst. Mom always managed to keep it away from me, and dad always pretended that the memory lapses never happened. I'd even gotten to the point of believing that his stay at this facility was only a temporary turn until the doctors could find another medication or equip him with some practical exercises that could be used to piece the fragments of his psyche back together whenever it came undone. So the picture that she painted of him right now was nearly impossible to process.

"Mom, it'll be okay. I'm coming right up."

"I'm telling you, you don't want to see him like this. Why don't you come back–"

She was interrupted by my knocking.

When I saw the expression of profound anguish on her face as she opened the door, I immediately cursed myself for not simply doing as she asked.

"What's going on? What's the matter with dad?"

"It's the disease, honey. This is who he is now. I'm sorry to tell you, but what you saw yesterday was the exception."

"Who in the hell is knocking at my door at this time of night?" The angry voice sounded nothing like my father's. "I told them to stop, damn it. Let them keep coming back. I'll have something ready they won't like one bit."

I felt a cascade of emotion rising in my chest that I worried I wouldn't be able to contain. "Why didn't you tell me he'd gotten this bad?"

Mom couldn't muster an answer. She merely looked at me with pleading eyes. "Just come back another time," she whispered over the loud grumbling from inside the apartment.

I looked inside and saw him sitting in the same chair that he'd been in yesterday, but his eyes were different. They were angry, distant, and very afraid.

I knew I couldn't leave without trying to bring him back.

"I'm sorry, but I have to see him," I said as I gently pushed past her and made my way inside.

The grumbling stopped the moment he saw me. He smiled as if overcome with relief, though his hazy eyes were still alien to me.

"Matty. Thank god you made it."

I turned to my mother, awash in confusion. "Does he think I'm..."

Dad answered the question for me. "Don't just stand there, Matthew. Sit down. We have a lot to talk about." The tone in his voice had leveled out to something I was more used to, even though everything else felt like a nightmare. I cautiously approached the chair next to him. He patted my knee with a heavy hand as I sat. "You're looking healthy."

I could feel my mouth quiver as I attempted to smile. "Thanks."

"Has that pinhead Brandt finally stopped giving you a hard time about your transfer out of SWAT?"

I nearly lost my breath. I quickly gathered myself enough to reply when my mom interrupted.

"Don't answer, Scott," she advised me. Then she turned to my dad. "Sweetheart," she said in the gentle, reassuring voice that kept our home life from imploding on countless occasions. "This isn't Matthew. Matty's gone. This is Scott."

When he looked at me, the mental fog that had momentarily lifted made an abrupt return. "I think I know my own son when I see him. Trust me, I haven't been drinking that much."

"You haven't been drinking at all."

"Yeah, well, all the more proof that I know what I'm talking about. Now would you mind letting me catch up with my boy?" Then he turned to me. "I hardly ever see you since you took that…" He didn't allow himself to finish the sentence. After a moment of labored contemplation, he looked at mom. "Can we have a few minutes please?"

The look on her face said that was the last thing she wanted to do.

"It's okay," I assured her. "We only need a few minutes."

I figured that playing along was better than confusing him more; not that I had the first damn clue about how to handle the situation. Mom clearly didn't share my less-than-expert assessment, but she begrudgingly walked into the bedroom and closed the door.

He stared at the door as if he'd fallen into a trance that he couldn't get himself out of. I nudged his shoulder, and he came back. When he did, his eyes had a renewed focus, and I held out hope that the fragments had somehow been pieced back together. But my hope was tragically short-lived.

"Are you sure about this, Matt?" he asked in a low, controlled voice.

His abrupt shift in tone threw me, and I hesitated to respond.

"There's a million and a half ways this thing can blow up on you. Taking a taste is one thing. That pretty much goes with the job. But this, what you're doing now... Jesus, your mother could never, ever find out. She'd kill you and me."

I swallowed hard, knowing now that I had to pretend to be my brother. "She won't find out."

He slapped me on the knee again. "Good. And as for the new guys they're bringing in, how solid are they?"

Play along, Scott. "Pretty solid from what I can tell."

"They'll have to be. There's too much to be lost for any of them to go into it half-assed. A score like that? It'll set you up for life."

"You and mom too," I said without thinking.

He met my response with a deep frown. "Be smart. Don't go throwing that shit around. That's the best way to give the dogs a scent."

I sat back in my chair and nodded; my stomach a queasy mess.

"Are any of the guys from SWAT?" he then asked.

"I don't know."

"Find out. And if there are, you watch them real good. Oliver Brandt is running a fucking cowboy outfit over there. It's ten times worse since you left."

I couldn't believe what I was hearing. It was almost too surreal. But it was happening, and despite everything in my body screaming at me to do otherwise, I had to let it continue.

"Does Brandt know about the score?" I asked.

"Of course he does. He helped set the goddamn thing up. And don't think he won't come asking for a cut when it's all over."

"I'll make sure I watch him."

"You watch all of them. Don't trust anyone but yourself."

"I will."

"And whatever you do, don't get yourself killed over this." His eyes suddenly began to water. "I can't lose you."

"I'll be okay," I said, wishing I really was able to speak for him. A heroin dealer killed Matt four years ago in an undercover buy gone terribly wrong. It was all part of a department-sanctioned sting operation according to the official story, but the dealer was tipped off prior to the transaction. When my brother's cover was officially blown, there was no back up to pull him out in time. The only solace we could take was that the dealer had been killed in a subsequent shootout with Matthew's fellow narcs.

I still had no idea where dad was going with this, but the more he talked, the more I was compelled to listen.

What he said next instantly changed that.

"There's one more thing I need you to do, Matty."

"What's that?"

"Keep all of this away from your brother."

"Of course." I managed the words, despite feeling like all the air had been sucked out of my body.

"Scotty can't handle stuff like this. He's not like us. He's too green and idealistic.

He waited for me to respond, but this time I couldn't.

"The boy has a good heart, and he's a cop for all the right reasons, but he can't see the forest for the damn trees. I know you've shown him things here and there when you can, so have I, but there's only so much we can do. And to be honest, I don't want to color this world for him. He's got to figure it out on his own. Your problem is that you're too much like me, which makes you a lost cause." He let out a quick laugh. "But Scott has a lot more of his mother in him. It could serve him, but it could also get him buried. Either way, he has to find his own path. But it can't be our path. Promise me you won't let him get sucked up in the shit like we did. Promise me you'll encourage him to be better every chance you get. That boy looks up to you, probably more than he looks up to me. You can make it better for him."

The sadness clogging my throat did not allow me to respond immediately.

"I need your promise, Matty. He's not one of us. He's better than us. We have to make sure he stays that way. Promise me he'll never know the other side of this. Of us"

At that moment, I understood what it felt like to utter your very last words. Everything you'd known your life to be would culminate in that split-second just before you spoke. Anything your life could've been would fall away immediately after you finished. I stretched the words out for as long as I could, knowing they'd be the last I ever spoke as Detective Scott Priest, proud son, proud brother, and careful steward of a family name that meant more to me than any title or position or accolade I could ever receive. After this, I'd become something else entirely.

"I promise, dad. He'll never know."

THE ROGUE
SHIELD

COMING IN 2018

Made in the USA
Middletown, DE
12 July 2021